THAT'S JUST THE WAY IT IS

"So," Stevie said, keeping her voice casual. "You must be pretty excited about seeing Sheila again, huh?"

"Sure," Callie said blandly. "It should be lots of fun. I can't wait."

"Really?" Stevie still kept her voice as neutral as she could. "That's cool. If it was me, I'd probably be kind of nervous."

"I guess," Callie said noncommittally.

Stevie plowed on. "I mean, friends are supposed to love you no matter what. But sometimes it's hard to remember that, you know? Especially if you haven't seen someone for a while."

Callie sighed. "Thanks for the pep talk, Stevie," she said, her voice weary. "I know you mean well and everything. But you probably shouldn't waste your time and energy on this one. Sheila and I have known each other for a long time. A really long time. I know things between us aren't exactly normal. But that's how they've always been, and at this point they're probably never going to change."

Don't miss any of the excitement
at Pine Hollow,
where friends come first:

PINE HOLLOW™

CONFORMATION FAULTS

BY BONNIE BRYANT

BANTAM BOOKS

NEW YORK • TORONTO • LONDON • SYDNEY • AUCKLAND

Special thanks to Sir "B" Farms and Laura and Vinny Marino

RL 5.0, age 12 and up

CONFORMATION FAULTS
A Bantam Book / April 1999

"Pine Hollow" is a trademark of Bonnie Bryant Hiller.

ISBN 0-553-49246-2

Published simultaneously in the United States and Canada

Bantam Books are published by Bantam Books, a division of Random
House, Inc. Its trademark, consisting of the words "Bantam Books" and
the portrayal of a rooster, is Registered in U.S. Patent and Trademark
Office and in other countries. Marca Registrada. Bantam Books, 1540
Broadway, New York, New York 10036.

PRINTED IN THE UNITED STATES OF AMERICA

OPM   0 9 8 7 6 5 4 3 2 1

My special thanks to Catherine Hapka for her help in the writing of this book.

ONE

"What are you doing in there, anyway?" Stevie Lake called impatiently, rapping sharply on the shower door. "Some of the rest of us stink, too, you know."

From behind the opaque fiberglass door, she heard her friend Lisa Atwood giggle. A moment later the door opened a crack, allowing a burst of steam to escape. Lisa poked her head out. "Sorry," she said. "The warm water just feels so good after our long ride. I'll be done soon. Promise."

"Okay." Stevie returned her attention to the old tavern mirror hanging above the two slightly chipped ceramic sinks in the long, narrow women's bathroom at Pine Hollow Stables. She stared at her own reflection, trying to decide whether she needed to wash her dark blond hair or not. After giving the ends a quick sniff, she decided she probably did. She, Lisa, and a group of their friends were going to dinner and a movie

1

in a little while, and Stevie knew that sometimes the scents of horse sweat, hay, and manure—sweet and comforting as they might seem there in the stable—weren't quite as welcome in the outside world. "Ugh," she muttered, giving her hair one last sniff. "That's what I get for spending two hours mucking out stalls before our trail ride. It's all Max's fault."

Lisa stepped out of the shower stall, a large white towel wrapped around her, just in time to overhear the last part of her comment. "What's Max's fault?" she asked.

Stevie slung a towel over her shoulder and grabbed the small mesh bag where she kept extra shampoo and soap for just such occasions as this. "It's his fault that I stink," she told Lisa, stepping into the shower but leaving the door slightly ajar so that she could continue the conversation. "Remember? I told you I got here early today to talk to Judy about Belle's inoculations, and Max put me to work."

"As usual," Lisa called back. "At least he's consistent."

Stevie grinned. Max Regnery, the owner of Pine Hollow, hated to see idle hands. From the first day new riders set foot in the stable, Max taught them that hard work was part of riding and that everyone was expected to pitch in. Riders not only groomed the horses they rode and cared for their tack, but they also were expected to contribute to the general upkeep of the entire stable. Sometimes they helped mix grain or sweep the floors. Other times, like today, they mucked out stalls.

Stevie peeled off her dirty riding clothes and tossed them onto the wooden bench where she had set her other things. Much like the bathroom itself, the shower enclosure was long and narrow, which meant there was a dry end and a wet end. Stevie went to the wet end and turned on the water, wincing slightly as the cold spray hit her.

Once she had adjusted the water to a comfortable temperature, she leaned toward the door opening to talk to Lisa. "What time does the movie start, do you remember?" she asked, raising her voice to be heard above the hiss of the shower.

"Not until eight," Lisa called back. "And it's barely six now. We'll have plenty of time to eat before we have to head over to the theater."

"Good," Stevie replied. "I'm starving. I just hope Phil doesn't eat all the food at the restaurant before the rest of us get there."

She stopped talking for a few minutes as she lathered her hair and rinsed it. Before long she was stepping out of the shower stall, feeling completely refreshed. A couple of hours of stable chores followed by a strenuous workout on the trail with her horse, Belle, had worn her out—but

3

only temporarily. No matter how tired she got, Stevie almost always managed to find enough energy for fun. And what could be more fun than spending the evening hanging out with her friends? *Especially Phil,* she thought with a slight smile. Despite the fact that Stevie and her boyfriend, Phil Marsten, lived in different towns and attended different schools, their relationship had only grown stronger over the years they'd been together. Stevie's friends sometimes teased her about that. In many ways she was an unlikely candidate for a successful long-term romance. She was headstrong, quick-tempered, opinionated, sometimes reckless, often stubborn. However, she was also intensely loyal—to her best friends, her family, her horse, and most definitely to Phil. Just a couple of months earlier, Stevie and Phil had celebrated their fourth anniversary of the day they'd met at riding camp.

Lisa was thinking about her own boyfriend, Alex, as Stevie stepped out of the shower. Lisa and Alex had known each other for years—ever since Lisa and Stevie had become friends, in fact, since Alex was Stevie's twin brother. For years Lisa and Alex had thought of each other as mere acquaintances. That was why everyone they knew—themselves included—had been so surprised when they'd suddenly fallen deeply in love the winter before. Now Lisa couldn't imagine how she had existed for so long without the constant comfort of Alex's love and support. He gave her life a wholeness that made every day a little brighter—a wholeness that had been sorely missing since her parents' divorce.

Lisa glanced at her watch. Alex would be there soon. He had learned to ride shortly after he and Lisa had started dating, but he still didn't spend nearly as much time at the stable as she did. "Have you seen Carole and Callie?" Lisa asked Stevie. "Shouldn't they be in here changing, too? I know I just said we have plenty of time, but only if everyone's on schedule."

"Don't worry about Callie," Stevie said, rubbing her hair vigorously with her towel. "I saw her on my way in here. She's already changed—she just wanted to spend a few minutes with PC before we go. She's probably finished by now."

"Good." Lisa was careful to keep her voice cheerful as she combed a straight part into her damp hair. She had shared her confused feelings about Callie Forester with Stevie just the evening before. Callie and her family had moved to Willow Creek, Virginia, a few months earlier, at the beginning of the summer. That was when things had started to change . . .

Lisa couldn't help sighing as she thought about everything that had changed in the past few months. She, Stevie, and their other best friend,

Carole Hanson, had been inseparable since the day they'd all met at the stable some four years earlier. Now they were in high school, with new responsibilities and busier schedules, but they had remained a tight threesome. Or they had until the Foresters came to town. Callie's father was a United States Congressman, and Callie herself was an accomplished endurance rider. Lisa had known that much before she'd left to spend the summer with her own father in California. What she hadn't expected was that the new girl would be partially paralyzed in a car accident, an accident in which Stevie had been driving, and that Callie would have to spend the entire summer learning to walk again.

The other thing that Lisa hadn't known before she left, or even suspected, was that Callie would become such good friends with Stevie and Carole. That had been a shock, especially when Lisa had first returned in late August. She was starting to get used to their friendship, but it still didn't come naturally to her to include Callie in their plans.

Stevie didn't seem to notice Lisa's thoughtful expression. She was busy trying to work a knot out of her thick, wet hair. "As for Carole, don't ask me where she is," she said, gritting her teeth as she yanked at her comb. "I guess she must be running early, too, because I haven't seen her since before our trail ride. She must've already showered and changed."

Lisa finished fussing with her own hair and turned to her small cosmetics bag. She didn't wear much makeup—just a touch of tinted lip gloss and a little mascara were all she really needed to bring out her large, almond-shaped eyes and healthy, glowing ivory skin.

As she stared into the mirror, she thought about the trail ride Stevie had just mentioned. "Today was fun," she said softly. "But I really wish I'd been able to ride Prancer. I miss her."

Stevie stopped struggling with her hair long enough to shoot Lisa a sympathetic glance. "I know," she said. "Like I said last night, I didn't really think much about it when I first heard that Max wasn't letting anyone ride Prancer. I mean, I guess I thought it was kind of weird, but I just figured it was one of those Max things, you know? But I can understand why it's freaking you out, especially since it's been, like, weeks and Max still isn't talking."

Lisa nodded, thinking of the beautiful mare she usually rode. *Used to ride,* she corrected herself with a little frown. *After all, I've only ridden her once in the past two months.*

When she thought about it straight out like that, she could hardly believe it was true. Before her summer in California, Lisa had rarely let more than three or four days pass between rides on the sweet bay mare, no matter how busy her schedule got. But after one trail ride upon her return in August, Max had suddenly banned everyone from riding Prancer. That had been annoying. For Lisa, part of the joy of riding was riding Prancer. Still, it had been the beginning of Lisa's senior year, and she hadn't had a whole lot of free time to spend at the stable anyway. So for a while she hadn't thought much about it.

But days and then weeks had passed, and Max still wouldn't tell anybody why the Thoroughbred was off-limits, although Lisa had asked him about it more than once. Max was a kind, understanding man most of the time, but when he didn't feel like talking, it was impossible to pry information out of him with anything short of a crowbar. Lisa had been forced to speculate and come up with her own theories. She'd tried to be optimistic for a while, but at this point it was becoming more and more difficult. She couldn't imagine anything innocuous that could keep a good school horse completely out of commission for so long.

Lisa tried not to think about any of that right now, since she knew there really wasn't much she could do about it. Her friends sometimes thought she worried too much, especially about things she couldn't control, and Stevie, in particular, had very little patience for thoughts and worries and

8

conversations that circled around and around without going anywhere. And that was exactly how Lisa's thoughts about Prancer seemed to work these days. For the past couple of days, especially, they had started revolving in a big circle, beginning with *It's probably nothing, just my imagination running away with me,* passing through *Maybe it's something minor, like a new training schedule or a pesky case of worms,* then on to *She's got a fatal disease and they don't want to tell me* before returning to *It's probably nothing* once again.

"Oh, well," she said, trying not to let her voice betray her concern. "I'll be too busy for the next few days to do much riding anyway. I have a big English paper due Tuesday that I've barely started. I'm going to be so swamped I probably won't even have time to wonder what's really going on with Prancer."

Stevie winced as her comb finally broke apart the last few stubborn strands of her knot. "Try not to worry about it," she advised Lisa. "It's probably nothing. I mean, everyone knows how you feel about Prancer—there's no way anybody around here would keep anything important from you. Especially Carole." She ran the comb quickly through the rest of her hair and flashed Lisa a reassuring smile in the mirror. "By the time you come out of your English-paper trance next week and want to ride again, she'll probably be back in rotation." She paused and frowned at her own reflection. "Unlike some other nonequine creatures I could mention."

"You mean A.J.?" Lisa guessed immediately. A.J. was Phil's best friend. A few weeks earlier, he had broken up with his girlfriend, Julianna, and virtually stopped communicating with his family and friends.

Stevie's frown deepened. "It's like I was telling you last night," she said. "I haven't actually seen him myself since all this started happening. So for a while I thought Phil was exaggerating when he'd tell me how strange he was acting."

"I know what you mean." Lisa tossed the lip gloss back into her bag. "We all thought A.J. was just upset about the breakup with Julianna, and Phil was upset because A.J. was upset."

"But then I saw Julianna," Stevie reminded Lisa. "She was *really* upset, and not just in the normal way people get after they break up. She didn't understand what had happened or why he was acting this way. She'd been sure things were going really well between them."

Lisa glanced at her friend understandingly. She and Stevie had gone over all this the evening before, but Lisa didn't mind listening again. *She cares a lot about A.J.,* Lisa thought as she zipped up her makeup bag and tucked it into her backpack. *She's trying to figure out a way to help him, find a logical reason for his behavior, so she's going over it and over it in her mind. Sort of the way I keep going over this Prancer thing . . . I mean I know it's not the same, but I can't stop worrying about her, just like Stevie worries about A.J. I only hope we're both worrying about nothing.*

Stevie met Lisa's eyes in the mirror and blew out a long, loud sigh of frustration. "I just don't get it. He's not acting like the A.J. we all know and love, and nobody can figure out why." Her face took on a more determined expression. "That's why I decided to go to his house after school Monday with Phil. I need to see for myself what's going on."

Lisa quickly leaned over and busied herself with repacking her things to hide a smile. *That's Stevie for you,* she thought fondly. *Whenever there's a problem, she wants to wade right in, see for herself, and find a way to fix it.* Then her smile faded as she thought about everything she'd heard about A.J.'s recent behavior. *Of course, that might not be so easy this time. If A.J. won't talk to Phil about whatever's bugging him, I doubt he'll talk to any-one—including Stevie.*

She stood up again and glanced at her friend, hoping that Stevie hadn't guessed what she was thinking. Stevie was busy packing up her own things in an old blue duffel bag, slinging her wet towel carelessly over her dirty clothes and soapy shampoo in a way that made neat and tidy Lisa cringe.

But Lisa had long since stopped trying to correct her friend's sloppy habits. "Almost ready to go?" she asked, determined to push all the troublesome topics out of her mind. She hadn't been kidding about that English paper—it was going to keep her busy for the next couple of days, so she might as well enjoy herself tonight.

"I'm ready." Stevie glanced at her unopened makeup bag on the edge of the sink. Then she gave herself a critical glance in the mirror. She smiled at her wet hair and steam-flushed damp skin. "The natural look," she declared, leaning over and impulsively kissing the mirror, leaving lip prints on the glass. "It's the only way to go!"

"I hear Callie," Stevie reported a few minutes later as she and Lisa walked down the stable aisle. "Sounds like she's in there."

She nodded to a doorway just ahead, which led to the student locker room. That was what everyone at Pine Hollow called the large, square room off the entryway. Unlike most other areas of the stable, which were dedicated primarily to horses, this room had been outfitted for the comfort and convenience of people. One wall of the room was lined with cubbyholes. Each of Max's riding students, from the tiniest beginner to elderly Mrs. Twitchett, who had to be at least eighty, was assigned one of the two-foot-square cubbies. Students could stow extra boots and riding equipment, schoolbooks, lunches, rain gear—anything that needed a place to stay while they were at the stable. Additionally, there were a few lockers for people who wanted a little extra security. A long, sturdy pine bench stretched most of the way across the room in front of the cubbies, and shorter benches flanked the other walls.

When Stevie and Lisa entered the locker room, Callie was seated on a bench, struggling to pull off one of her high riding boots. Stevie winced slightly as she watched the other girl bending awkwardly over her own feet, her forehead creased with determination. Callie had come a long way in the months since the accident, but at times like this, when her body had trouble performing what would have been a relatively simple movement for anyone else, it was obvious that she still had a way to go. Stevie's guilty feelings had mostly faded by now, but she still wished the whole thing had never happened, that Callie had never been hurt. That feeling would probably never fade, at least not until Callie was able to walk again without the aid of the sturdy crutches lying on the bench beside her.

Callie's brother, Scott, was leaning against the

wall nearby, watching his sister. "Let me help you with that," he said, stepping forward with a look of concern on his broad, handsome face.

Callie frowned at him. "I've got it," she said stubbornly. She adjusted her grip on the boot and gave a quick yank. Her face twisted briefly in discomfort, but a moment later the boot was off.

Stevie shook her head, half in admiration and half in amazement. Callie was really something. High leather field boots like Callie's could be difficult to get off without the help of a friend or a boot jack, even for someone without Callie's physical difficulties. Stevie herself usually preferred to wear cowboy or low jodhpur boots whenever she didn't plan to do much jumping, though she knew that Callie probably needed all the ankle support she could get for her weak right leg. Still, it was just like Callie to see needing help getting her boots off as a sign of weakness rather than a basic necessity. She was one of the most independent and strong-willed, and stubborn, people Stevie had ever met.

Stevie didn't say anything about what she was thinking to Callie, though. Along with her other qualities, Callie was a very private person. Stevie sometimes had trouble understanding that—especially when her boundless curiosity crashed into Callie's naturally aloof, sometimes slightly suspi-

14

cious personality—but she had learned to respect it.

"So," she said cheerfully instead, "are you guys ready to try the best onion rings in the entire state of Virginia?"

Scott turned and grinned. "Hi, Stevie. Hi, Lisa. I didn't hear you two come in. I'm starving! I'd forgotten how long it takes to get you guys away from your horses."

Stevie returned his smile, still a little amazed at how easily it came. Until just a few days earlier, she had believed that she and Scott would never be friends. He had been very angry about his sister's injuries in that car crash, and even though the accident hadn't been Stevie's fault, he had blamed her because she was driving. He had snubbed Stevie for months whenever he saw her—first at Pine Hollow, where Callie came regularly for therapeutic riding sessions, and then more recently at Fenton Hall, the private school all three of them attended. But they had finally worked out their problems, and now Scott was his normal, outgoing, charming self around Stevie again.

Callie leaned over to tuck a pair of boot trees into her boots, then straightened up and grabbed her crutches. "Where are we going for dinner?"

"A place on the far side of town called Hank's Bank," Stevie said. "They call it that because the building it's in used to be a bank. I think you'll like it. It's cheap, and the portions are huge."

"Sounds great." Callie smiled. "I'm famished. Emily worked me hard today." Emily Williams was another friend. She had been working with Callie ever since the accident, guiding her recovery through therapeutic riding on Emily's own well-trained horse, PC. Emily knew a lot about therapeutic riding from her own experience. She had been born with cerebral palsy and had to use crutches or a wheelchair on the ground. On horseback, however, her physical disability seemed to disappear and she could do almost anything her friends could do. Emily's friendly and generous nature had made her eager to share the freedom and physical benefits of therapeutic riding with Callie, and since Callie had been a rider before the accident, it hadn't been a hard sell at all.

Scott rolled his eyes and smiled fondly at his sister. "Right, blame Emily," he joked. "You're the one who insisted on working twice as hard as usual because you're taking a couple of days off for Sheila's visit."

Stevie shot Scott a quick glance, searching his face for any trace of sarcasm. Even though she couldn't detect any outward signs, Stevie knew that Scott didn't like Callie's best friend from back home—he thought she was shallow and pretentious. Sheila was visiting the East Coast to tour some colleges, and she was stopping by on her way back to spend time with Callie.

"Listen, that reminds me." Callie didn't bother to respond to her brother's teasing. She glanced at Stevie and Lisa. "Sheila's arriving on Monday afternoon, and I'd love for you all to meet her. I was thinking we could have sort of a little welcome party for her at my house Monday after dinner. What do you say?"

Stevie shrugged. "Sure, sounds like fun."

She guessed Callie was nervous about her friend's visit. Scott had confided that Callie and Sheila had an unusual relationship. They had known each other since they were little and had stayed close even though Sheila was a year older. But somehow they had never really learned to open up and be honest and supportive. Instead they competed in all sorts of ways, subtle and not so subtle, and challenged each other constantly, each trying to be better than the other. Stevie was sure that was why Callie wanted all her new friends around for Sheila's first night. She was afraid to face her alone because she hated the thought of appearing weak in front of her—and to Callie, not being able to walk without her crutches was a sign of weakness.

"How long is Sheila staying, anyway?" Stevie added, trying to sound casual. She had already decided she wanted to help Callie and Sheila become truer friends—Callie deserved that—and she needed to know how long she had.

"She can only stay through Wednesday evening," Callie reported. "She's got one more interview up in Pennsylvania first thing Thursday, then she's heading home right after that."

Lisa looked surprised. "Wow, that's not a very long visit."

Stevie nodded. She would have to work fast. But she was sure she could do it. Callie had been a bit prickly when she'd first arrived in Willow Creek, but she had changed a lot in the past few months. Her accident had forced her to rely on people and trust strangers in a way Stevie doubted she ever had before. Because of that, Callie was more open these days, quicker to accept new people and ideas. Stevie hoped that meant she was ready to try a new way of relating to her oldest friend—a better, more honest way.

"I wish she could stay longer," Callie said. "But now you see why I want to make sure you all meet her right away."

"Well, I can't promise anything," Lisa said. "But I'll definitely come if I finish my English paper in time."

"Good." Callie smiled. "Oh, and make sure you invite the guys, too. I already mentioned it to Carole when I saw her earlier."

"Hi, everyone," a new voice interrupted. "Sorry I'm late."

Lisa turned to see Alex's familiar tall, lanky form strolling into the locker room. "You're not late," she assured him with a smile, jumping up and hurrying over to give him a welcoming kiss.

He kissed her back warmly, wrapping both arms around her waist and pulling her close. Lisa closed her eyes and felt herself sinking into the kiss. She forgot where she was for a moment, what she'd been doing. . . . Everything in the world suddenly faded away except her and Alex and their wordless communication—

Stevie let out a loud wolf whistle right behind Lisa's left ear.

"Sorry." Lisa blushed and pulled away from her boyfriend. "It's just that Alex and I haven't seen each other all day."

"Ah, young love," Scott said drolly, patting his heart with one hand.

As Alex sat down on the bench next to Stevie, she gave him a friendly punch on the shoulder. "Anyway, your girlfriend's right," she said. "You're not late, for once. We're still waiting for Carole and Emily."

"No, you're not," Emily's voice sang out from the doorway. "Emily's here."

"Okay, I stand corrected," Stevie said cheerfully as Emily entered, swinging along expertly on

19

her crutches. "Now we're just waiting for Carole." She glanced at her watch. "And as of now, she's officially late."

Lisa checked her own watch. "Only by about thirty seconds," she said. "We've still got a little time to spare—Phil isn't expecting us until six-forty-five. Let's give her five minutes or so. You know how she can be." Lisa smiled as she said it. Carole had always been the most serious of all of them about horses. She planned to work with horses as a career someday, and around the stable, she was totally responsible, organized, and efficient. However, those qualities didn't always cross over into the rest of her life. "She's probably rushing around making sure every last horse in the stable is comfortable enough to survive without her for a few hours."

Emily laughed. "You're probably right," she agreed, lowering herself onto the bench beside Scott. "When it comes to horses, Carole never does anything halfway."

Ten minutes later, Stevie checked her watch for the fifth time. "Okay, that's it," she declared. "If we don't get going soon, we'll have to gulp down our food without chewing if we want to make it to the movie. We'd better go find Carole."

"Maybe she's getting changed," Callie suggested.

Stevie nodded. "Good thought. Let's check the bathroom and the office first." Carole, unlike the others, no longer had an assigned cubby in the locker room. Since she worked part-time at Pine Hollow, she was allowed to store her things in the old metal cabinet behind her desk in the stable office.

A quick check of bathroom and office failed to turn up Carole. The group gathered once again just outside the locker room.

"Now what?" Lisa glanced anxiously at her watch.

"I guess we'd better search the place," Alex said with a shrug. "I mean, we know she's here somewhere, right?"

"Miraculously enough, my brother's right," Stevie agreed briskly. "Let's split up and check all the usual spots—Starlight's stall, the feed shed, the outdoor ring . . ."

Suddenly she noticed a new figure lurking in the hall near the tack room. It was Ben Marlow, Pine Hollow's youngest full-time stable hand. Stevie had never really understood Ben. He was a little too mysterious, a little too dark and brooding for her taste. But he definitely knew what he was doing when it came to horses, and she respected him for that. She also knew that Carole was probably the closest thing Ben had to a friend.

21

If anyone knew where she was right then, he might.

Emily was obviously thinking the same thing. "Yo, Ben," she called. "We're desperately seeking Carole. Have you seen her lately?"

Ben, as usual, appeared surprised that someone was speaking to him. He cast Emily a quick glance from the corner of his eye, then jerked his chin toward a set of large wooden double doors across the way. "Did you check the indoor ring?"

"The indoor ring?" Stevie repeated. "What would she be doing in there at a time like this? She's supposed to be getting ready to meet us."

But Scott cocked his head and listened. "It does sound like someone's in there." He hurried over to the doors and pulled one open to peer inside. "Aha!" he said. "Call off the search. We found her."

The others hurried to see for themselves. When she pushed her way past Alex for a better look, Stevie couldn't believe her eyes. There was Carole, riding through a small jump course on Samson, a horse she was training for Max, as if she didn't have a care in the world!

Stevie waited as patiently as she could until the big black horse landed safely at the end of the course. Then she stepped forward. "Carole!" she called sharply.

Carole looked up from beneath the rim of her

hard hat, an expression of surprise on her face. "Oh, hi, Stevie," she said, pulling the big gelding to a prancing halt. When she noticed the others hovering in the doorway, her brow furrowed. "Um, what are you guys doing here? I'm sort of in the middle of—"

"Carole! I can see what you're doing, but what you're supposed to be doing is getting ready to go." Stevie's voice was even sharper this time. It was obvious what had happened: Carole had gotten so caught up in what she was doing that she had completely forgotten about their plans. It wasn't the first time she had done something like this, and Stevie couldn't help feeling annoyed. "It's almost six-forty-five. Phil's waiting for us at Hank's. We're supposed to go to the movies, remember?"

A look of dismay dawned in Carole's dark eyes. "Oh, no!" She glanced at her watch. "I totally forgot."

"Obviously," Scott said with a laugh.

Lisa was fidgeting, shifting her weight from one leg to the other. "Hurry up, okay?" she said, a hint of anxiety in her voice. Everyone knew that Lisa hated to be late. "We've got to get going."

"I'll never be ready in time," Carole said helplessly, glancing down at her mount. "I'd have to cool Samson down, and groom him . . ." Sud-

23

denly her eyes lit up hopefully. "Hey, do you think we could go to a later showing?"

Stevie glared at her. Carole could be awfully aggravating when she got like this—when she forgot that anything could be more important than her duties at the stable. But Stevie tried to hold on to the last few scraps of her patience as she responded. "There is no later showing," she said. "Eight o'clock is the last one tonight. That's why we planned things this way, remember?"

It was obvious from the look on Carole's face that she *didn't* remember. "Sorry," she said sheepishly. "Look, why don't you go ahead to the restaurant without me? Maybe I can finish up here and meet you at the theater."

"Don't be silly," Emily said. "Why don't you let Red or Ben cool Samson down for you? One of them must owe you a favor or two."

Carole shook her head. "But it's not just Samson. I'm supposed to bring in those two yearlings from the west pasture before the evening feeding. And I haven't exercised Starlight yet today at all." Starlight was Carole's own horse, a tall bay gelding her father had bought her for Christmas several years earlier.

"Maybe we could help you," Emily said uncertainly, leaning over to check Stevie's watch. "If we all pitch in . . ."

Callie was standing near the back of the group.

She was feeling a little impatient. Carole was one of the nicest, most down-to-earth people she knew, but she could be a tad flaky. Right then Callie could almost feel the seconds and minutes ticking away as everyone tried to come up with a solution to Carole's forgetfulness. Callie's father sometimes teased her by claiming she had a mind like a steel trap and a personality to match. When she decided to do something, Callie *always* remembered—and did it. She didn't really understand people who forgot things they were supposed to do, lost track of the date or time, canceled plans, and changed their minds constantly about what they wanted. She couldn't imagine stumbling through life that way.

She felt, rather than heard, someone come up behind her. Turning, she saw Ben standing there. She was a little startled—he was so quiet and inconspicuous that she hadn't realized he was still hanging around in the doorway.

When he saw Callie looking at him, Ben gave her what he probably thought was a smile, though to Callie it looked more like a pained grimace. "Carole lost track of time, huh?" he said.

Callie didn't answer for a second. Granted, she had only known Ben for a few months, but she couldn't remember another time when he had voluntarily engaged in small talk—with her or anyone else. Besides that, it wasn't clear whether

25

the remark had actually been directed to her, since Ben was now staring thoughtfully at his own feet. "Looks that way," she said at last.

Ben looked up again, seeming startled to receive an answer. "Carole's been doing that a lot lately," he muttered. "Losing track of stuff."

Once again, Callie wasn't sure how to respond. Luckily she was saved from having to figure it out. Their conversation was cut off as Stevie brushed between them. "I'll call Phil at the restaurant," she called over her shoulder. "He's probably there by now. He'll have to meet us at the theater instead, and we'll eat afterward."

"Wait!" Carole called after her. "You don't have to do that. Why don't you guys just go ahead? Really. I don't mind. I can see the movie another time."

"Don't be silly." Lisa glanced around at the group and started ticking things off on her fingers in her usual organized way. "Now, come on. You can start cooling down Samson while Alex and Scott and I head out and round up those yearlings. Emily and Callie can clean your tack . . ." Her voice trailed off. "Oh. Then there's Starlight. Maybe we can just turn him out in the paddock or—"

Ben stepped forward. "Don't worry about him." His voice was quiet, but it carried easily to the whole group. "I'll longe him for you if you want."

Carole shot him a grateful look. "Oh, that would be great, Ben," she said as everyone turned to look at him. "Thanks."

Ben shrugged, looking slightly uncomfortable at the attention. "No problem."

Lisa took a step toward him, smiling tentatively. "That's really nice of you, Ben," she said. "And listen. If you're not too busy tonight, we're all going to the movies and then out for a bite to eat. Would you like to join us?"

At that, Ben looked more uncomfortable than ever. He glanced helplessly over his shoulder, like a cornered animal searching for a safe exit. "Um, I don't think so," he muttered. "I have a lot—I mean, I have to—I don't think so."

Callie shook her head as Ben turned and fled. He was a strange one, that was for sure. But she didn't have much time to think about it. She had some tack to clean.

TWO
2

"If I faint, don't try to revive me," Alex declared, clasping his stomach dramatically and sliding down in his seat. "Just shove some food down my throat and I'll be fine."

Carole lowered her menu and glanced across Hank's Bank's largest table, where the entire group of friends had just been seated. The restaurant was packed with its Saturday-night crowd, which included adults and younger children as well as other high-school students. "Sorry," Carole said for at least the fifteenth time. She knew it was her fault that they were eating three hours later than any of them had planned. Her friends hadn't let her forget it—they had been teasing her nonstop since they'd all left the theater earlier.

Carole understood her friends' teasing, after all, because she was used to it. She knew as well as anyone that she could be scatterbrained when it came to anything other than horses. To her, though, that was only natural. Somehow the things other people found important, things like school, social events, time, even food and sleep, tended to fly straight out of her head whenever she got engrossed in her work at the stable—the work she loved better than anything else, and which she fully planned to devote her life to as soon as she finished school.

Lisa elbowed Alex in the ribs. "Enough," she ordered. She knew that Carole wasn't particularly sensitive to teasing, but she was afraid they might be going a little overboard. After all, they were here now, all together and ready to eat. That was what really mattered. "If you don't stop teasing Carole about this," she warned her boyfriend playfully, "I may have to ask Stevie to start telling stories about what you were like as a little boy."

Stevie grinned and sat bolt upright. "Sure!" she said eagerly. "I could start with the Halloween when we were four and I decided to dress up as a mermaid and Alex got jealous of my cool costume and made Mom and Dad get him one just like it. Or maybe you'd rather hear the one about when he decided he wanted to join a nudist colony when he was five and—"

"Okay, okay!" Alex protested, holding up both hands in surrender. "I get your point. Carole, you won't hear another peep out of me all evening. Not even if the police question me about why all my friends suddenly dropped dead of starvation."

Everyone laughed at that, including Carole. Then the group turned to a discussion of the movie they had just seen, until the waitress interrupted. "Ready to order, kids?" she asked cheerfully.

"Are we ever!" Phil declared. "Just bring us one of everything."

"Make that two of everything," Alex corrected.

Stevie rolled her eyes at the guys. "Pigs," she said. Then she turned to the waitress to place her order.

Everyone else followed suit, and before long the waitress was hurrying off toward the kitchen. Lisa leaned back in her seat, hoping the food would come quickly. She was really hungry, despite having shared a large popcorn with Alex at the movies.

To take her mind off her grumbling stomach, she glanced at Callie, who was sitting across from her. Lisa still felt slightly awkward being around Callie, but she was smart enough to know that the only solution to that was for them to get to know each other better. "How did your riding session go today?" she asked politely.

"Pretty well, thanks," Callie replied.

Emily, who was sitting next to Callie, grinned. "Really well, she means," she told Lisa. "Callie and PC are getting along so well, I'm starting to feel jealous—like maybe his real name is something like Perfect for Callie."

Lisa laughed. When she, Stevie, and Carole had first met Emily, she had kept them on their toes by constantly making up new names to fit her horse's initials, from Prince Charming to Personal Computer.

Lisa's mind wandered, unbidden, to yet another phrase that fit PC's initials—Prancer Can't, as in "Prancer can't be ridden." Despite her determination to forget about everything serious and have fun, she was finding it hard to dismiss that particular issue. Lisa liked to have answers to her questions. That was one of the things that made her a good student and a fast learner. The flip side of that quality was that at times like this, when she couldn't get the answer she really needed, it tended to gnaw at her, making it difficult to concentrate on other things. And it was getting harder and harder to sit back and be patient about Prancer's situation. She had managed for a while, theorizing that Judy Barker, the equine vet who was half owner of Prancer, might be selling her share in the horse to Max. Beyond that, Lisa's imagination ran wild. There were plenty of things that could go wrong with a horse's health, and some of the possibilities were very frightening indeed—and by now Lisa had considered all of them. Still, none of it made sense, and she knew that worrying wouldn't help.

Lisa forced her attention back to Callie and Emily's discussion. They were planning Callie's training sessions for the next couple of weeks.

". . . and once your friend leaves and we're back on our daily schedule, we can take it from there," Emily was saying.

Callie nodded. "Sounds good." She looked worried. "Do you think missing three days in a row is going to make a big difference? I mean, maybe I could work something out so we could—"

"Oh, please!" Emily exclaimed. "I bet you could miss twice that long and have no problem at all picking up where you left off." She turned and winked at Lisa across the table. "If I don't watch out, Callie's going to get so good at this that she won't need me anymore."

Callie smiled at Emily. "Not a chance," she said. "There's no way I could have come this far without you."

As Lisa listened to the other two girls, she fiddled with her spoon. Part of her realized that what Callie had just said was rather unusual. Lisa didn't know Callie well, but she knew her well enough to sense her strong will and independent spirit. It was probably a pretty big deal for her to admit how much she counted on Emily. Still, Lisa understood perfectly. She knew from talking to Carole and Stevie that Emily had been a good friend and a patient partner in Callie's recovery since the beginning.

I just wish Emily could help me with my problem, she thought sadly. *I wish she could help me believe that there's nothing seriously wrong with Prancer. Because if I don't get some good news pretty soon, it's going to drive me crazy.*

At the other end of the table, Scott and Phil were deep in a discussion of the finer points of the Washington Redskins' defensive line that season. Stevie sipped her water and listened patiently as long as she could stand it. But finally she'd had enough. She liked sports as well as the next person, but she had trouble comprehending how people could discuss the same things about their favorite teams or games over and over again.

"Okay, that's enough," she said abruptly. When the two guys glanced at her in surprise, she went on briskly. "Time for a new topic. Otherwise I'm going to die of boredom even before I die of hunger." She glanced down the table at Carole to see if she'd heard the gibe, but Carole was busy talking to Alex.

Scott looked a little surprised at her interruption, but Phil just saluted sharply. "Aye-aye, ma'am," he said in his best military voice. "Orders understood and obeyed. What would you care to talk about at this time, ma'am?"

Scott chuckled at that. "I see you have your boyfriend well trained, Stevie," he joked.

Phil grinned. "Watch what you say," he told Scott. "If you're not careful, I'll sic her on you. Then you'll be sorry."

"Very funny." Stevie rolled her eyes. "Now if you don't mind, let's try having an intelligent conversation about something that doesn't involve shoulder pads and end zones, okay?"

"Fair enough," Scott said good-naturedly. He shot Phil a quick, mischievous grin. "Why don't you get us started, Stevie? I'd love to hear your views on world peace. I always find your insights extremely fascinating."

Stevie sent him a sour glance as Phil laughed. "Is that one of your junior politician's tricks to make me think you're not some boring, sports-obsessed nut?" But she couldn't keep her eyes from twinkling with amusement. Now that she and Scott were talking again, she was remembering why she had liked him in the first place—and realizing why he and Phil were rapidly becoming good friends. Scott sometimes did come across as the younger version of a smooth-talking politician like his father. He was rarely at a loss for an appropriate response to anything anyone said, and he had a way of making people feel comfortable with him no matter what the situation. But he was also warm and genuine underneath that slick, handsome exterior, with a sharp and slightly wicked sense of humor and a quick and lively mind.

"You'd better watch out, buddy," Phil said, grinning. "It's not going to be easy to get Stevie's vote. She's a cynic."

"Ha ha." Stevie stuck her tongue out at her boyfriend.

Scott chuckled. "Good thing I won't be running for any offices at Fenton Hall," he said, reaching for his water glass. "Stevie might decide to run against me."

Stevie just grinned at that. Privately, she thought it was too bad the election for student body president at her school had been held the previous spring, before Scott came to town. *If he had been around then, maybe we wouldn't be stuck with prissy little Trina Sullivan as our president,* she thought, thinking of the perky, popular senior who had won by a landslide. *If I'd known she was going to win and torture us with her stupid ideas about new cheerleading uniforms and fat-free ice cream in the cafeteria, I really might have considered running against her myself.*

"Maybe we should have a coup," she said half seriously. "We could take Trina and the rest of her clique hostage and threaten to take away their makeup and feed them nondiet soda until they give in to our demands."

Scott shrugged. "I'm game," he joked. "But only if you'll sign on as my head general and bodyguard."

At that moment the waitress headed toward them carrying a large platter heaped with food. Another waitress followed with a second tray.

"Aha!" Alex crowed. "We're saved!"

Carole sat back and watched as the waitresses quickly and expertly passed out plates of burgers, sandwiches, and salads, accompanied by tall, frosty glasses of soda and juice. At the end, with a flourish, they set two large platters of fresh, hot onion rings in the center of the table.

Reaching for an onion ring, Carole glanced around the table at her friends. Stevie, Phil, and Scott were in the midst of a lively discussion—or was it an argument? Sometimes with Stevie it was hard to tell, since she seemed to enjoy arguing with people, including Phil, almost as much as she liked a friendly chat. Lisa, meanwhile, seemed to be lost in thoughts of her own as she munched on the tuna melt she had ordered. Next to Lisa, Alex was eagerly discussing with Callie and Emily the merits of onion rings versus french fries, so Carole sat back, popped the hot, greasy onion ring into her mouth, and allowed her mind to drift back to her favorite subject—horses.

Horses always occupied a large part of her mind, but lately one horse in particular had dominated her thoughts. Samson had come to Pine Hollow just a few short weeks before—twenty-seven days, nine hours, and fifty-five minute before, as Carole could have told anyone who asked, after just a moment or two of calculation. But this wasn't the first time the big, athletic black horse had lived at the stable. Actually, he had been born at Pine Hollow—his dam, a beautiful palomino named Delilah, had been one of Max's most popular school horses, while his sire, Cobalt, had belonged to a wealthy rider Carole's age named Veronica diAngelo. Veronica had been a good rider, but she had been careless, more concerned with appearances and getting what she wanted than with safety. Because of that, there had been an accident, a tragic accident that had resulted in Cobalt's death.

Carole had been very attached to Cobalt, and his death had been a hard blow. For a while, in fact, she had seriously considered giving up riding altogether. It had seemed too difficult for her to face the idea that accidents could happen, that the life of such a beautiful, vibrant creature could suddenly be taken away with no warning whatsoever. That a noble, regal creature could suffer and die, and that there was little or nothing Carole could do to prevent it.

That was why Carole, even more than her friends, had been so touched by Samson's birth a few months later. Even from the beginning, the colt bore a remarkable resemblance to his sire, from his gleaming black coat to his fiery spirit. For Carole, that had been an unmistakable sign that Cobalt's soul lived on even though his body had died, and for that reason, along with his own special personality, Samson had always been a particular favorite of hers.

As he grew up, Samson had shown signs of great talent as a jumper, and eventually Max had sold him to a serious rider in the next county who had hoped to take the big black horse to the Olympics someday. For a while, Carole had all but forgotten Samson, thinking of him mostly on special days, like his birthday or the anniversary of Cobalt's death.

Then Max had announced that Samson was coming back to Pine Hollow. Carole had been thrilled about that, and even more thrilled when Max had asked her to take over Samson's training.

Carole still wasn't sure exactly what she wanted to do when she got older. Sometimes she thought she might want to be a competitive rider; at other times she considered becoming a riding instructor and stable owner like Max or a vet like Judy Barker. But whatever she did in the future, Carole knew that training experience would come in handy. Good riders never stopped training their horses, reinforcing and adding lessons even on a simple trail ride. For that reason, Carole took every training task seriously. But training Samson was extra special, not only because of her feelings for him, but also because he had real potential to be a champion show jumper.

As Carole methodically ate her burger and onion rings, she thought back over her progress with Samson for the past week and planned how to proceed in the days and weeks to come. The horse was so talented that it seemed there was nothing he couldn't do—it was just a matter of having her help him reach his potential. It was a challenging task, but one that completely fascinated and absorbed her. The only drawback was that there just didn't seem to be enough hours in the day for her to spend with the wonderful black horse . . .

At that same moment, Lisa was once again trying to force her worries about Prancer out of her mind. She reached for an onion ring, her hand colliding with Stevie's over the platter as they grabbed for the same one.

"Watch it," Scott joked. "You'd better back off. Stevie seems pretty serious about these onion rings."

Lisa laughed. "No kidding," she agreed. "I've seen her fight her own mother for the last one on the plate. More than once, actually."

"Guilty as charged," Stevie said. "But tell the truth, Lisa. Now that you've tasted Hank's onion rings again, aren't you extra glad you didn't decide to stay in La-La Land this year after all?"

Lisa's breath caught in her throat, and she felt her heart stop dead in her chest. It started beating again half a second later, twice as fast as usual, as she glanced at Alex sitting beside her. When she saw that he was leaning forward, talking earnestly with Emily about his favorite rock band, she let out a quick sigh of relief. Thank goodness. He hadn't heard Stevie's comment.

Lisa pushed back her chair quickly. "I'm going to make a run to the ladies' room," she said as casually as she could manage. "Stevie, want to come along?"

"No thanks," Stevie said without looking up from her plate. "I don't need to go."

Lisa grabbed Stevie by the shoulder. "Come on," she said pointedly. "I could use some company."

Stevie looked up at her in surprise. "Well, okay," she said uncertainly. She glanced at Phil and Scott and grinned weakly. "You know us girls," she joked. "We can never go to the rest room alone. It's like a rule of the universe or something." She shoved one more onion ring into her mouth, then got up and followed Lisa through the restaurant to the bathrooms.

Once they were safely inside, Lisa checked the stalls to be sure they were alone and then turned to Stevie. "Do you realize what you almost did?" she asked, exasperated.

Stevie was confused. She could see that Lisa was upset about something, but she didn't have the slightest idea what it was. "Um . . . ," she said blankly.

Lisa leaned against a sink and rubbed her face. "Sorry," she said. "I guess there's no way you could know."

"Know what?" Stevie was still lost. "What did I do? What's wrong?"

Lisa bit her lip. "It was what you said out there. About me almost staying in California." She hesitated. "Um, you see, I never quite got around to telling Alex about that. He doesn't know I even considered not coming back to Willow Creek."

Stevie gasped, truly surprised. She had been as amazed as everyone else when her brother and Lisa had gotten together. The two of them hadn't seemed to have much in common at first—aside from Stevie herself, of course. But they shared a basic kindness and honesty that more than made up for any minor differences in interests or opinions. That was why it was so hard to believe that Lisa could have kept something so important from Alex for this long. She had long since explained to Carole and Stevie how she had seriously considered spending her senior year in California, living with her father and going to school out there, instead of returning to Willow Creek High School, her mother, and the rest of her life here. Stevie had assumed that Lisa had talked over this decision with Alex, too. Apparently she was wrong.

"You haven't told him?" she blurted out. "Why not?"

Lisa shrugged and picked at her fingernails. "I meant to," she said. "It just hasn't been easy to find the right time. I mean, he's been kind of weird about the whole subject of California."

Stevie frowned. "Well, okay," she said slowly. "I guess he did have a little trouble with that. But you're back now. And he deserves to know the truth."

"I know." Lisa gave Stevie a pleading look. She knew it couldn't be easy for Stevie to be caught in the middle like this, her loyalty to her twin struggling against her loyalty to her best friend. "And you're right. I really do have to tell him. It's just— I need a little more time. Please?"

Stevie felt decidedly uncomfortable with this whole conversation. She and Alex didn't make a big deal out of the fact that they were twins. But the truth was, deep down they really did share a special bond, a kinship that was different than what Stevie felt with her two other brothers.

Keeping something this important from him just didn't feel right. Knowing that Lisa hadn't told Alex about her decision was almost as disturbing as it would have been to find out she had been keeping a secret from Stevie herself.

Still, Stevie understood Lisa's position. Alex hadn't exactly been reasonable about the prospect of spending the entire summer apart from his girlfriend, and he would probably have some trouble accepting the idea that Lisa had even considered extending that time. "All right," she said reluctantly. "I guess we'll all be a lot better off if you can find a way to tell him so that he doesn't totally freak out. But please—make it soon."

Lisa smiled with relief. "I will," she said. "Thanks, Stevie. I really appreciate this."

Stevie shrugged. "It's okay," she said. "But listen, it's just blind luck this hasn't slipped out before now. I mean, Carole knows everything, too. And I mentioned it to Phil." Seeing Lisa's look of dismay, she quickly added, "I'll tell him not to breathe a word. But you're on your own with Carole. You know how hopelessly honest she is."

"I know," Lisa said. "I'll have to talk to her about it right away. I think she'll understand if I explain the situation."

"Probably," Stevie agreed. "Anyway, you probably don't have to worry that much about her. She never talks about anything but the stable these

43

days, so there's not a lot of danger she'll say anything incriminating."

At that moment the rest room door opened and Callie stuck her head in tentatively. "Hi," she said. "Um, sorry if I'm interrupting anything."

"You're not," Stevie said. "Come on in."

Callie limped in, holding her left arm out in front of her carefully, with both her crutches in her right hand. Stevie could see that the sleeve of Callie's blouse was soaked with what she assumed was soda.

"What happened?" Lisa asked.

Callie smiled and shook her head. "It's no big deal," she said. "Alex got a little overexcited about something Phil said—something about the Redskins and the Eagles, I think—and spilled his drink all over the place. Mostly on me."

Stevie rolled her eyes. "Typical," she said. "He's always been a clumsy oaf."

"I'd better go help clean up." Lisa grabbed a handful of paper towels from the dispenser near the door. "See you guys out there." She disappeared through the door, leaving Stevie and Callie alone.

Stevie gave Callie a sidelong glance as she leaned over the sink to rinse her sleeve. This was the perfect opportunity to talk to her about Sheila's visit.

"So," she said, keeping her voice casual. She

didn't want to give away the fact that Scott had told her about Callie's relationship with Sheila. "You must be pretty excited about seeing Sheila again, huh?"

Callie kept her gaze trained on her sleeve. "Sure," she said blandly. "It should be lots of fun. I can't wait."

"Really?" Stevie still kept her voice as neutral as she could. "That's cool. If it was me, I'd probably be kind of nervous." She gestured at Callie's crutches, which were leaning against the sink. "Especially if I wasn't feeling quite like my normal self, you know?"

Callie shot her a quick glance in the mirror. "I guess," she said noncommittally.

Stevie plowed on. "I mean, friends are supposed to love you no matter what. But sometimes it's hard to remember that, you know? Especially if you haven't seen someone for a while."

For a second Callie seemed disinclined to respond. But finally she glanced up again. "That's true," she admitted softly. "But you can't let nerves stop you, right?"

Stevie could tell that, as usual, Callie wasn't eager to open up about her private thoughts and fears. But she also suspected that Callie was just nervous enough about the impending visit to really listen to what Stevie was saying instead of cutting her off with one of her none-of-your-business glares or a sharp word.

"You can talk to me about this, you know," she said impulsively. "That's what friends are for."

Callie frowned, looking startled. "Um, thanks," she said uncertainly. "But it's no big deal, really. Sheila and I—well, we've been friends for years. But not in the way you and Carole and Lisa are. I mean, if it was you with these"—she waved a hand at her crutches—"they'd be, you know, supportive. I'm not so sure how Sheila will react." She shrugged. "So if I'm a little nervous, that's the reason."

That was the opening Stevie had been waiting for. "But just because things have been a certain way in the past, it doesn't mean they always have to be that way," she said eagerly. "Maybe if you give her a chance to understand by really opening up and trusting her, everything will change. You could have a whole different kind of friendship. A better one."

Callie sighed as she dried her arm with a paper towel. "Thanks for the pep talk, Stevie," she said, her voice weary. "I know you mean well and everything. But you probably shouldn't waste your time and energy on this one. Sheila and I have known each other for a long time. A really long time. I know things between us aren't exactly normal." She tossed the used paper towel into the bin under the sink. "But that's how they've always been, and at this point they're probably never going to change."

She moved toward the door without another word. Stevie shrugged and followed. It was clear that Callie had had enough of this topic for the time being.

But that didn't mean Stevie was giving up.

THREE

Callie stared into the mirror that covered one entire wall of Cosmopolitan Cuts, keeping a close eye on the stylist who was clipping cautiously at the ends of her long blond hair. Callie had only been there a few times and still didn't quite trust the employees to follow her instructions about her hair. She sighed, suddenly homesick, as a vision flashed through her mind of her salon back home, where her regular stylist had known exactly how she liked her hair done, from the length of the cut to the scent of the shampoo she preferred. On top of that, Callie was feeling uncomfortable about being in the salon at all. It was, after all, Sunday afternoon, and normally Cosmo Cuts would be closed. However, Mrs. Forester had phoned the salon's owner, explaining that she needed her hair styled for a big luncheon she had to attend the next day at which the First Lady would be one of the guests, and he had agreed to open just for her and Callie. Sometimes

48

it made Callie uncomfortable to get this kind of special treatment, but her mother took it all in stride. And her mother was careful not to take advantage of her position and to always thank people who went out of their way to help her. Still, Callie wondered if she could ever get used to the attention.

She pushed those thoughts aside and, with a concerted effort, looked away from her reflection in the mirror long enough to check on her mother's progress.

Mrs. Forester was sitting in the next chair, her face and arms relaxed, looking as completely at home as if she had been born and raised in this salon and never known anyplace else. Callie never ceased to wonder at that ability. Her father and brother had it, too. They rarely, if ever, felt uncertain and out of place, as Callie herself did all too often. Somehow, though, this talent was most impressive in her mother. Maybe it was because Mrs. Forester and Callie bore such a strong resemblance to each other. Aside from thirty-odd years, a few pounds, and different hairstyles, the two could have been twins. But more than that, Callie always found it amazing that her mother could simultaneously take control of a room and slip into the background, giving center stage to her husband or whoever else was present—in this case the salon owner, Charles, who was working on her neat blond bob. Mrs. Forester had a way of making people feel appreciated and important, from ordinary people on the street to egotistical people like Charles. Callie knew that was a valuable talent for a politician's wife, but she still didn't understand how her mother did it.

Sensing her daughter's gaze, Mrs. Forester turned to smile at Callie. "Oh, Pierre!" she exclaimed, widening her smile to include Callie's stylist. "You're doing a wonderful job on Callie's hair."

"Your daughter is so beautiful, she needs little help," the stylist replied in his thick French accent, bowing slightly toward Mrs. Forester.

Callie just sighed. She was used to having people fawn over her because of who her father was, but that didn't mean she liked it. Ignoring Pierre, she glanced at her mother. "Is Dad going to drive me to the airport tomorrow to pick up Sheila?"

"I spoke to him." Mrs. Forester smoothed the apron that protected her stylish silk pantsuit from hair clippings. "He really hoped he'd be able to do it—you know how fond he is of Sheila—but he's afraid his new committee is going to need him tomorrow afternoon." She smiled up at Charles, who was hovering above her with a bottle of mousse. "A congressman's work is never done, you know," she told him confidingly, with a disarming smile. She returned her attention to Callie.

"I spoke with your brother. He'll be happy to drive you."

Callie frowned. She knew that Scott had never liked Sheila much. He was good at hiding his feelings, but she could usually read him even when others—including their parents—couldn't. Still, she guessed there was no other option. Mrs. Forester would be at the luncheon until late afternoon, and Callie couldn't drive herself because of her leg.

"All right," she said with a barely perceptible sigh.

Mrs. Forester was smiling at herself in the long mirror. "It's so nice that Sheila can stop by on her college tour," she commented contentedly. She glanced at Charles. "My daughter's best friend from our old hometown is coming for a visit."

"Isn't that nice!" Charles cooed, shifting the mousse bottle to his other hand and continuing his work.

"I'm sure she and Scott will be glad to see each other, too." Mrs. Forester tossed Callie a playful wink. "Don't you remember when you were all in elementary school, how the two of them used to pretend they were getting married?" She glanced up at Charles. "Sheila had the prettiest little white dress she would wear, and she would put on some lovely music . . ."

Callie winced as her mother went on. She re-

51

membered those "weddings" all too well. For a period of several months, Sheila had insisted on playing that particular game at least once a week. And since Scott was the only "groom" available, and since he and Callie were siblings, naturally Sheila always got to play the bride. Callie was stuck being the minister every time.

Of course, I got my revenge for all that when I took the blue at our first Pony Club rally, she reminded herself. *Especially since all she got was a "good effort" ribbon.* Callie smiled with grim satisfaction as she remembered the look on Sheila's face when Callie had walked forward to accept her ribbon and trophy. That had really put Sheila in her place for a while. *She pretended it was no big deal, just like I always pretended not to care about being the minister, but—*

Suddenly Callie caught herself. What was she doing? Her oldest, dearest friend was arriving the next day, and all she could think about was their petty childhood rivalries.

Of course, those rivalries were always a pretty big part of our relationship, she thought ruefully. *And now . . .*

She glanced at the shiny metal crutches leaning against a nearby counter. Just for a moment, she found herself desperately wishing that things could be different. If only she hadn't been in the car that day. If only the accident had never happened . . .

She shook her head, causing Pierre to jerk his scissors back and shoot her a dirty look in the mirror. But she ignored him, too distracted by her thoughts to worry about her hair. She knew better than to waste much time on wishing things were different. What had happened had happened, and now she had to deal with the consequences.

Maybe there's still a way to make up for all that, though, she told herself. *Even Sheila has got to see that this is temporary.* She glanced at her crutches again. *Especially if I convince her that the rest of my life here in Washington is positively fabulous.* She smiled at the thought. *I mean, even Sheila would probably be impressed with all the famous politicians I've met since we moved here, like that handsome young senator who came to visit me when I was in the hospital.* She pursed her lips. *And then there's Fenton Hall. It's really a pretty impressive school, much more prestigious than our boring old public school back home.*

Callie frowned again, suddenly disgusted with herself. What was she doing? Sheila was coming all the way across the country to see her, and before she even arrived Callie had an attitude about it. What was wrong with her, anyway? Maybe Stevie had a point. Maybe it *would* be better if she grew up and broke out of those ridiculous old patterns. After all, Sheila was her best friend, wasn't she? They had known each other all their lives, for better or worse. If Callie couldn't be honest with Sheila, whom could she trust?

That wasn't a comfortable thought. Callie trusted Sheila as much as she trusted anybody, but she still didn't relish the thought of risking her pride by appearing less than perfect, less than completely in control, in front of her.

Still, what do I have to lose? she told herself. *Sheila lives way across the country now. The worst that can happen is I'll humiliate myself and she'll get her jollies telling everyone back home what a loser I've become.*

That wasn't a pleasant thought at all, but Callie forced herself to face it down. She had no reason to think that Sheila wouldn't welcome a new beginning. The only thing she had to fear was her own inability to make it happen.

All I can do is try, she thought with sudden determination. *I'll try to be a real friend to Sheila for a change. I just hope I can figure out how to do that.*

She glanced at her mother, who was chatting graciously with Pierre about his hometown in the south of France. It would be nice to talk to someone about Sheila. But somehow Callie didn't think her mother would understand. Maybe she could ask Stevie for some pointers. She certainly seemed to be interested in helping.

That's what I'll do, she decided, nervously squeezing the armrests of the stylist's chair but already feeling better. *I'll call her as soon as I get home.*

At that moment Carole was in Starlight's stall at Pine Hollow, giving him a quick grooming.

"Hold still," she told the big bay sternly as he shifted his weight and took a step forward. He was a little frisky, and for a moment Carole felt guilty. She had ridden him for about half an hour in the small back paddock, but it hadn't really been enough exercise after his light workout with Ben the day before.

Still, it's not really my fault, she told herself. *Red needed the big paddock for that colt he's breaking, and Max had a class in the main ring. . . .*

She put it out of her mind. Starlight would survive, and she had other things to think about right then. She was trying to figure out what to do with Samson. She'd been planning some simple conditioning hill work in the rolling north meadow, but the previous day the gelding had been a little difficult to handle, and she was afraid he was getting bored with all the flat exercises and grid work she'd been doing with him lately. Like people, horses liked some variety in their routine, and Carole knew that with a spirited, intelligent horse like Samson, it was especially important to keep him interested in his work. She had been spending almost half their time on jumping—it was hard to resist, since Samson was in such superior physical condition that he probably could have jumped every day with little problem—but now she realized that the horse must need a real break from his serious training.

Sort of like a minivacation, she thought as she grabbed a soft brush out of her grooming kit and set to work on Starlight's face. *He needs a change of scenery. Something that will be fun and interesting for him, to refresh him and get him back in the mood for work.*

Starlight snorted and jerked his head slightly as she moved the brush a little too close to his eye. "Oops. Sorry, boy," she said automatically, patting him and switching to the other side of his face. But she wasn't really seeing Starlight standing there in front of her. She was picturing Samson, trying to figure out the best course of action for that day's session.

I haven't done that much cross-country or trail work with him, she thought. *That's probably a mistake. He needs to have varied enough experience to prepare him for any strange-looking jump a course designer can come up with in the show ring.*

Carole nodded thoughtfully as she slowly

brushed Starlight's cheek. In show jumping, course designers used a variety of methods to test the horses that would be attempting their course. Besides varying the distances between obstacles and adding other challenges such as combinations or water elements, the designer could also create unusual-looking, odd-shaped jumps to test the horse's concentration and obedience to its rider. Samson would have to be ready for all that when he returned to the show ring, and viewing plenty of unusual, unexpected, even frightening items in the real world—fallen logs, natural streams, manmade gates and walls—was one way Carole could help prepare him.

Carole stood on tiptoes so that she could see over Starlight's head and down the aisle to the main door. It looked just as sunny and pleasant outside as it had been an hour before when she'd been out with Starlight. *That's what we'll do today,* she decided, feeling pleased. *A nice leisurely trail ride will be a break in routine for both of us. And if we take the mountain trail, I can even get in some of that hill work I was planning.*

She smiled at that thought. The mountain trail, which snaked through the woods and climbed a series of steep hills to a high, rocky spot with a fantastic view of the surrounding woodland, was one of her favorites out of the many trails near Pine Hollow. Exploring it with Samson would be an absolutely wonderful way to spend a gorgeous sunny afternoon. In fact, she couldn't think of anything she'd rather do.

"Okay, Starlight," she said, giving her horse's face one last quick swipe with the brush. "I think we're just about done here."

She tossed the brush back into the grooming bucket and glanced around the stall. She had mucked out a few minutes before and there was a fresh flake of hay in his hayrack, so all she had to do was refresh the water bucket hanging in the corner and she would be free to go tack up Samson for their ride.

She slung the grooming kit over one arm and grabbed the water bucket with her other hand, grunting slightly under its weight.

"Guess you weren't too thirsty today, huh, boy?" she commented to Starlight. She knew his light workout probably had something to do with that, but again, she pushed that out of her mind.

She ducked under the webbing at the front of the stall and set the grooming bucket down, then hoisted the water bucket and started down the aisle toward the faucet at the end of the U-shaped stable area, doing her best not to slosh water on her clothes.

"I don't know why Max doesn't just put in automatic waterers," she muttered. "Practically every other stable around here has them, and it would sure make things easier for all of us—not to mention keeping us a lot drier." It was tempting to dump the water out right where she was instead of carrying it all the way over to the drain beneath the faucet, but she knew Max frowned on that. She peered down at the water in the bucket. It didn't look as though Starlight had taken more than a sip or two since she had filled it earlier that day. For a change, there weren't even many stray specks of hay or straw floating on the top. Usually Starlight was a slob when it came to drinking, polluting his bucket with bits of whatever he had been eating or sniffing at most recently.

As Carole staggered around the corner and came in sight of the faucet area, she also came in sight of Ben Marlow. He was standing in front of the faucet watching a burly older man in a tool belt tap at the pipe leading up from the cement floor.

"What's going on?" Carole asked, lowering her bucket carefully.

Ben looked up. "Drain's clogged," he reported in his usual succinct manner. His dark eyes shifted to the bucket at Carole's feet and he shrugged. "You'll have to use the sink in the tack room for now."

The plumber glanced up at Carole over his shoulder. "Don't worry, miss," he said in a deep, cheerful voice. "It's nothing serious. I'll have this baby fixed in no time. Half an hour, tops."

Carole weakly returned his smile. "Okay," she said. "Um, thanks." With a groan, she reached down and hoisted Starlight's water bucket once again.

Great, she thought impatiently as she started the long trek back down the aisle. *Just my bad luck.* Now she had to traverse the entire length of the stable aisle, passing Starlight's stall halfway down, then cross the entryway and go down another hallway to the tack room. It wasn't really very far, but just at the moment, with a full water bucket that felt heavier with every step—not to mention a mind full of eager plans for her ride with Samson—it seemed miles away.

She glanced around furtively, suddenly realizing she was alone in this part of the stable. She could move a lot faster if she just dumped out the old water right here. Nobody would ever know. And as she had noted, the water was relatively clean. She was sure Starlight didn't have any communicable diseases. What would be the harm?

Just as she was about to tip the water onto the dirt floor, Starlight stuck his head out of his stall and pricked his ears toward her. When she saw him, a new idea popped into her head. She glanced once more at the water in the bucket.

It really is almost perfectly clean, she told herself.

60

I mean, it would probably get more dust and dirt and gunk in it in the walk from the tack room than is in there right now. Maybe I should just return it as is and be done with it.

The idea was tempting—very tempting. Max normally insisted on having the water for all his horses changed at least three times a day. But Carole knew that a lot of other horse owners didn't bother with that. If they didn't have automatic watering systems, they simply checked their horse's water supply throughout the day and changed it as necessary.

And right now, it's not really necessary, is it? she thought, taking another few steps toward Starlight's stall. *Besides, Starlight isn't Max's horse. He's mine. I should be able to judge when his water needs replacing.*

She nodded, mostly satisfied with that logic. Ignoring the quivering speck of doubt in the back of her mind, she set the bucket down outside the stall and unhooked the webbing. Then she bent down to pick up the bucket one more time. However, as she lifted it and stepped forward into the stall, pushing aside Starlight's inquisitive nose with her shoulder, she caught a flash of movement out of the corner of her eye.

She gulped, suddenly feeling irrationally guilty. *Don't be ridiculous,* she assured herself as she hurried across the stall to place the water bucket in its usual spot. *You're not doing anything wrong. Besides, what you saw was probably just another horse sticking its head out over the door.*

But as she gave Starlight a quick pat and stepped past him and out of the stall, she saw that it hadn't been a horse after all. Ben was walking down the aisle toward her, staring her way with a surprised expression on his face.

Carole felt her face grow hot as she swung the wooden stall door shut behind her. She couldn't believe her bad luck. Ben had seen her going into Starlight's stall with that water bucket—and he would have known there was no way she could have gone to the tack room and back so fast. He must have guessed exactly what she had done.

"Hi," he said as he reached her. He stopped and glanced over her shoulder into Starlight's stall.

"Hi," Carole muttered in return, not quite meeting his eye. She grabbed the grooming kit, which was still sitting where she had left it. "Well, see you."

Ben didn't respond, and Carole was careful not to look back as she fled down the aisle toward the tack room. She wasn't sure why she was so embarrassed. It wasn't as if Ben had caught her doing anything truly bad. So why had he looked at her as if he had?

I guess he's just Mr. Perfect, she thought sullenly. *Well, not everybody can be Superstablehand all the time, like him. If he doesn't like that, it's his problem, not mine.*

She sped around the corner, out of range of what she imagined was his disapproving gaze. Only then did she allow herself to relax and slow her pace. She wanted to forget about the encounter with Ben. There were too many other things to think about. More pleasant things. Starting with tacking up Samson . . .

FOUR

The clash and clatter of flatware against crockery and the smack of plastic trays against wooden tables filled the air as Stevie strode across Fenton Hall's cavernous tiled cafeteria. Balancing her tray on one hand, nodding to acquaintances, she headed straight for the table at the far end where she usually sat.

When she got there, she found Callie already seated with her bag lunch in front of her. That was no surprise, since Callie sat in the same place almost every day. What was unusual were the other occupants of the table.

"Hi," Stevie said to Callie, taking the empty seat across from her and shooting a questioning glance at the three girls in the surrounding seats.

Callie rolled her eyes. "How's it going?" she said. "Um, Betsy and Nicole and Moira decided to sit with us today."

"Oh." Stevie gave the trio a polite smile. She had known Betsy Cavanaugh, Nicole Adams, and

64

Moira Candell for years—Betsy had even ridden at Pine Hollow for a while back in junior high. But in her memory, none of them had ever chosen to sit with her at lunch. They generally preferred the more rarefied air of the table in the center of the room, where all the wealthiest, snobbiest, and in Stevie's opinion most irritating juniors and seniors gathered every day.

Stevie sighed in annoyance. *Of all the times for Betsy and her friends to go slumming!* she thought sarcastically. She'd been hoping to get some time alone with Callie to discuss Sheila's arrival that afternoon. Callie had called her just before dinner the day before and admitted for the first time exactly how anxious she was about seeing Sheila again. She had also said that she'd been thinking about Stevie's comments on Saturday night and had decided to give her advice a try. She wanted to forge a new kind of relationship with her oldest friend, a more honest and open one.

Stevie had been thrilled. She'd spent the next few minutes discussing the best ways for Callie to put this plan into action, and now she was dying to continue their conversation. Unfortunately, even though both of them were juniors, the only class they had together was phys ed, and that was only two days a week. That was why Stevie had had such high hopes for this lunch period. But from the look of things, they weren't going to get a moment of privacy.

She shot a disgruntled look at Betsy and her friends, who were busy discussing the fat content of Moira's salad dressing. "Sorry I couldn't talk long last night," Stevie told Callie. "For some reason, my brother Michael was totally berserk about using the phone." She rolled her eyes. "He's really getting weird lately. Mom says I was just as bad when I was thirteen, though I find that impossible to believe."

"That's all right. You told me everything I need to know." Callie smiled at her, wishing she could say more. Stevie's brief advice truly had been helpful. Just talking with Stevie had been inspiring in itself. Callie had been really nervous about confiding her thoughts about Sheila, but Stevie had been incredibly understanding. What's more, she had seemed eager to help coach Callie through the next few days.

Now if these three airheads would just leave us alone, we could get down to business, Callie thought irritably, gritting her teeth as Nicole let out an earsplitting squeal of laughter at something Moira had just said. *What in the world are they doing here, anyway?*

Normally she would have assumed the girls were hanging around because they were impressed by her father's job and, by extension, Callie her-

66

self. She was used to that. She had put up with that kind of unjustified fawning at her old school back home. But she had purposely kept a low profile since starting the year at Fenton Hall. Of course, most of the students had probably at least heard of her, both because of her well-known last name and also because of the news coverage of the previous summer's accident. But Congressman Forester had been careful not to let any recent photos of his daughter get into the press, and that had allowed the naturally reserved Callie to retain some anonymity among her schoolmates so far. She had known that would change eventually, though, and now it seemed as though it was happening sooner rather than later.

Of course, Scott might have something to do with it, she reminded herself. *He's never been exactly bashful about getting acquainted, and it won't take long for all his new friends to figure out that I'm his sister . . .*

As if reading her mind, Betsy suddenly turned toward her with a peppy smile. "So anyway, Callie," she said brightly. "We were just wondering. Did Scott have a girlfriend back home?"

With considerable effort, Callie held back a snort. She should have known. These girls were exactly the type who were drawn to her brother like moths to a flame. Unfortunately, she also guessed from similar experiences that they were the type who wouldn't be brushed off easily. Callie could be as cold or as sullen or as openly hostile as she wanted, and they would still hang around until they had the information they wanted from her.

"Not really," Callie replied, unwrapping the carrot sticks her mother had packed for her and avoiding the other girls' eager, attentive eyes. "I mean, he dated a few people. But nothing serious."

"Oh!" Betsy smiled. "Good. Do you know if he's going to the Willow Creek High football game on Saturday?"

"What's the matter, Betsy?" Stevie asked sarcastically. "Don't tell me you got tired of Kenny Lamb already."

Moira wrinkled her nose and gave Stevie a derisive glance. "Get real," she drawled. "Betsy dumped that loser weeks ago. Everyone knows that."

Stevie rolled her eyes, and Callie sighed. She had been steeling herself for Sheila's arrival all day, but she hadn't realized how much she'd been counting on a last-minute pep talk from Stevie to get her through. Now it was obvious it wasn't going to happen.

Nicole leaned forward to gaze earnestly at Callie. "So what's it like living with such a gorgeous older brother?" she asked in her breathy, soft voice. "It must be so awesome. Especially if all his friends are gorgeous, too."

Moira smirked. "Actually, I heard he's hanging out with kind of a weird crowd," she commented, looking at Stevie slyly out of her carefully made-up green eyes. "I even heard he invited Stevie's boyfriend to play tennis a few times."

Nicole's eyes widened. "Really?" she asked, sounding truly amazed. "That is weird. Did you see them there?"

"No," Moira replied. "But Veronica did. She said that Scott must be doing some sort of charity work with the clueless." She shot Stevie a fake little smile. "No offense."

Betsy scowled at her friends. "Who cares what Veronica thinks?" she retorted a bit peevishly.

Stevie held back a snort. She knew that in that particular group of girls, everyone cared what Veronica diAngelo thought. She had been the self-declared leader of the clique for as long as anyone could remember.

Stevie shot Callie a frustrated glance, wishing Betsy and her gaggle of annoying friends would leave them alone to talk. But then she sighed, realizing it was hopeless. *I guess Callie will just have to figure it out for herself,* she thought. She knew that Callie was more than capable of that, but she still wished she could help. Now all she would be able to do was show up at Callie's house that night with everyone else and see how it was going.

She grimaced as Nicole and Moira started arguing over whether Scott looked like some hunky TV star or not, and Betsy tried to charm her way into Callie's good graces. Stevie played idly with her soup spoon and tried to figure out exactly how many days of detention the headmistress would give her if she dumped her lunch tray over Betsy's head.

Whatever the answer, she decided, it wouldn't be worth it. *I should probably thank my lucky stars that all my brothers are such total nonstuds that I never have to put up with anything like this.* Despite her increasingly sour mood, Stevie couldn't help grinning at the thought. Her smile faded as she glanced at Callie again. The other girl looked miserable. *I guess I really am lucky,* Stevie thought more seriously. *It can't be easy being Callie sometimes.*

A little later that day, Carole was daydreaming about Samson as she walked through the crowded hallways at Willow Creek High School. Their trail ride the day before had been positively wonderful. Samson had really seemed to enjoy the change of pace, and it hadn't taken Carole long to realize how much she was appreciating the break, too. She had been awfully busy lately. Not only had she been putting in her usual several hours a day at the stable, but her father, a retired Marine Corps colonel, had been away for the past week giving lectures at several corporate retreats in the Midwest. That meant Carole had also been responsible for rustling up her own meals and doing her own laundry.

And of course, there's always school getting in the way of things, Carole added glumly.

She was so deep in thought that she wasn't paying much attention to where she was walking as she rounded a corner of the hall. "Hey!" a familiar voice said. "Watch where you're going."

Carole looked up, startled, and saw Lisa's smiling face in front of her. "Oh," she said. "Sorry. I guess I'm a little distracted."

"I'll say." Lisa turned and walked beside Carole as she continued down the hall. "Thinking about anything interesting?"

Carole shrugged and grinned sheepishly. "The usual," she admitted. "Horses."

"Big surprise there," Lisa joked. The two girls took a few more steps in silence; then Lisa spoke again. "Um, listen, Carole," she said. "Speaking of horses, there's something I've been wanting to talk to you about."

Carole looked at her in surprise, wondering why she suddenly sounded so somber. "Shoot," she said.

71

"It's . . . Well, it's Prancer," Lisa said, standing still.

Carole stopped, too. She should have guessed. "Prancer?" she repeated as innocently as she could. "What about her?"

"Well, I'm sure you know Max has her off-limits," Lisa said, clutching her books to her chest. "I haven't been able to ride her since school started."

"Oh, you know Max." Carole forced a carefree little laugh. She was determined to head off this line of questioning right away, before Lisa pried the truth out of her. It had been hard enough for Carole to keep Max's secret this long. She didn't want to ruin the surprise now. "He can be pretty mysterious sometimes, but you don't have to worry. He always has a good reason for stuff, right?"

"I guess so." Lisa didn't look convinced.

Carole's mind was already wandering. Her own words had reminded her of how secretive Max had acted a few years back when he'd been negotiating to sell Samson. "He's the boss," she mused, remembering how sad she had been when Max had finally announced that Samson would be leaving. "That means sometimes he's got to be the one to make the big decisions."

Before Lisa could answer, someone called her name. Carole turned and saw Gary Korman, a tall, soulful-looking boy with large brown eyes and a perpetual slouch, coming toward them. "Yo," he said with a glance at Carole. "How's it going?"

"Not bad," Carole replied automatically. She didn't know Gary very well—he was a senior, like Lisa—but she had always liked him well enough. He played bass guitar in a local band and had a laid-back way of dealing with the world that she admired.

Gary was looking at Lisa with an expression approaching panic on his usually tranquil face. "Yo, Lisa," he said, holding up a tattered notebook. "You know those physics problems we were supposed to do this weekend? I'm totally lost. Can you give my paper a quick check and see if I got any of the answers right at all?"

"Sure." Lisa gave Carole a slightly worried look. "Maybe we can talk about this later, okay?"

"Sure. See you." Glancing at her watch, Carole realized that she had less than a minute to get to her history classroom for seventh period. Then there was eighth period and Spanish III, and after that, she would finally be free—for one more afternoon, at least.

She hurried down the hall and scooted through the classroom door just as the bell rang. Her history teacher picked up a pile of papers from her desk as Carole and the other students scrambled for their seats.

Carole dropped her backpack on the floor beside her chair and slumped down behind her desk, already counting the minutes until class was over. It took her a moment to notice that Ms. Shepard was distributing the papers she was holding.

"Welcome, everyone," the teacher said as the class quieted down. "I trust you all had a restful weekend. But not *too* restful, of course."

Several of the other students tittered nervously. Carole wrinkled her brow in confusion, not understanding the teacher's comment or her classmates' laughter.

She got the joke a moment later when one of the papers landed on her desk. As soon as she looked at it, the letters at the top of the first page seemed to leap up at her and slap her sharply on the face: TURN-OF-THE-CENTURY AMERICA: EXAM, CHAPTERS FIVE THROUGH ELEVEN.

Carole gasped. A test? She couldn't believe it. Searching frantically through her mind to Friday's class—had it really been only three days ago?— she tried to recall any mention of an upcoming test. But all she could remember about that class period was that it was when she had decided Samson could use some refresher work over cavalletti in the coming weeks.

She bit her lip and glanced again at the test in

front of her. Chapters five through eleven—had she read those? She was pretty sure she had read chapter five sometime last week . . .

The first ten questions were multiple choice. Some of them even covered material that sounded vaguely familiar. Carole picked up her pencil and got started.

A few minutes later, she had answered six of the ten and was fairly confident that most of the answers were right. Deciding to come back to the last four questions later, she flipped to the second page.

Uh-oh, she thought, feeling her heart sink. *Essay questions.*

There were five of them. As she scanned the first one, her heart sank even more: "Describe what turn-of-the-century philosopher George Santayana called the Genteel Tradition, and explain the forces that opposed it in the early years of the twentieth century."

Carole bit her lip. She definitely didn't remember anything that sounded like that from chapter five. Still, the other four essay questions didn't look any easier, so she decided she'd better just plunge right in and hope for the best.

She read the question again, trying to focus. *The Genteel Tradition,* she thought. *That sounds like something Mrs. Atwood would like.* Before her divorce, Lisa's mother had spent a lot of time trying to turn Lisa into what she called a proper young lady. One of her favorite words was *genteel,* and Carole was pretty sure it meant something similar to *proper. Here goes nothing,* she told herself grimly, gathering her thoughts as best she could. Calling to mind a vision of Mrs. Atwood as she had been before her divorce, she began.

"The Genteel Tradition was the idea that there's only one proper way to do things," she wrote, clutching her pencil so tightly she was afraid she was going to break it. Forcing herself to relax, she went on writing. "The people who believed in it thought they knew what was genteel and what wasn't. For instance, they thought they knew the best way to dress, the proper foods to eat, the correct books to read, and so forth. They didn't like it when anyone disagreed with them. But some other people opposed their ideas and wanted things to change."

Carole paused, trying to figure out how long her answer needed to be. She was running out of ideas for this particular question, though she had the nagging feeling that she wasn't getting it quite right.

"The upper classes believed in the Genteel Tradition," she wrote. "They didn't want things to change because any change could only be bad for them. A lot of them didn't even care if poor people couldn't afford food or new clothes or even hay for their horses."

She smiled, feeling rather proud of herself for working in that reference to horses. One thing she did remember from reading chapter five was that horses were still the primary means of transportation at the turn of the century.

Just imagine, she thought, lowering her pencil for a moment. *It wasn't even that long ago—just a hundred years, give or take. And almost everyone relied on horses for their daily life. Horses pulled carriages, plows, fire engines. They carried the mail, went into battle during wartime, herded cows and sheep, hauled lumber. They were the original public transportation in cities and the precursor to the tractor on the farm.*

Her mind boggled at the thought of all those horses, everywhere, helping human civilization to run.

And now, not all that much later, she added to herself, resting her chin on one hand thoughtfully, *most people in the United States don't so much as set eyes on a horse from one day to the next.*

In a way, that was even harder to believe. Carole couldn't imagine going one day without the company of horses. Saddling up a pony for a younger rider, mucking out Starlight's stall as he watched with his ears pricked forward in that way he had, swinging herself into Samson's saddle and feeling his eagerness to take her anywhere she wanted to go . . .

She sighed wistfully, wishing she could be sliding her foot into Samson's stirrup right that moment. He was such a special horse. She had known that from the day he was born, but he proved it again and again every minute that she knew him. She knew that Max was expecting great things from Samson someday soon. The big black horse had the talent, the speed, and the fearless, determined character to be a real contender in the show-jumping ring. Carole planned to help him reach that potential.

That reminded her of their trail ride the day before. She had noticed something that troubled her a little—Samson had hesitated slightly when she'd asked him to ford the creek that crossed the trail in one spot. It had only been a momentary hesitation, after which the big horse had splashed through the broad, fast-moving, shallow stream with no further problems. But Carole knew that even such a minor thing could signal trouble in the future. She had known of at least one champion show jumper with a fear of water. In fact, she had watched a competition on television just a few months earlier in which that very phobia had cost the horse and its rider a ribbon. Not every course included a water jump, but this particular one had, and the horse had refused the jump once and then knocked down a rail when his rider rode him to the obstacle again. Those had been the pair's only faults, but they had been enough to keep them out of the jump-off.

Carole didn't want to take the slightest chance of having a problem like that develop with Samson. She was determined to head off any nervousness the horse felt about water before it could take hold.

I don't think he was really scared, she thought, chewing on her eraser as she went over the scene at the creek slowly in her mind, trying to pinpoint what Samson's reaction had been to the bubbling brook. *I think it was just something new and strange that he wasn't expecting. He probably won't think twice the next time he encounters water on the trail.*

She mentally chastised herself for taking a different way home the day before, one that didn't involve fording the stream. Now she would have to wait and wonder.

Still, she wasn't too worried. Samson was spirited and sometimes impulsive, but under it all he was an intelligent and sensible horse. She was sure she could cure him of any minor water phobia he might have. All it would take was patience and understanding, much like any other part of training . . .

She was still thinking about that when a shrill sound jolted her out of her musings. It took her

79

half a second to remember where she was—sitting in history class—and another half second to recall what she was supposed to be doing.

The test! she thought in a total panic. *I forgot all about the test!*

She felt like kicking herself. She couldn't believe she had sunk so deep into her daydreams that she had completely lost track of reality. Class was over, and most of the questions on her paper were still unanswered. She could hardly believe it. Usually class seemed to last forever, but somehow that day the time had passed in what felt like the blink of an eye. Now the bell had rung and the other students were already hopping out of their seats, gathering their books, and hurrying forward to drop their test papers on Ms. Shepard's desk.

Carole flipped back to the first page and frantically scribbled random answers to the remaining multiple-choice questions. She gulped as she peeked at the second page again, the one that seemed glaringly white with the answer space for four of the five essay questions still blank.

But it was too late to do anything about that now. Crossing her fingers and hoping for a miracle, Carole stood and shuffled toward the front of the room with her test paper clutched in her hand.

FIVE

Later that afternoon Lisa pulled into her driveway and coasted to a stop. Glancing at the garage, she saw her mother's car inside. That meant Mrs. Atwood wasn't working that day—her shifts at the clothing store where she was assistant manager generally ran either from eight-thirty to four or from two to ten, which meant that if she was home when Lisa got home from school, she was home for the whole day.

Lisa climbed out of the car and hurried toward the back door, already planning her evening in her mind. She really wanted to finish her English paper in time to meet everyone at Callie's house at eight. Luckily she had made a lot of progress the day before—she had spent most of the day in the tiny public library in downtown Willow Creek and the evening planted in front of the computer in her bedroom. Another bit of luck was that her other teachers hadn't assigned much homework for the night, thanks to a quiz in her Spanish class, a substitute in calculus, and a two-part lab in physics.

She let herself into the kitchen, noting the breakfast dishes still sitting in the sink and the scattering of crumbs on the table that meant her mother had probably eaten cheese and crackers for lunch again. Lisa shook her head, wondering once more why life sometimes seemed so unfair. Back when her parents had still been married, Mrs. Atwood had been . . . well, maybe not happy, exactly, but content in her own way, while Mr. Atwood had been miserable. He had hidden it reasonably well at the time, but after seeing how happy he was with his new wife and baby in California, Lisa knew that the difference was dramatic.

The difference had been equally dramatic for her mother, but in the opposite direction. Since the divorce, Mrs. Atwood had sunk into a morass of bitterness, regrets, and recriminations, refusing to accept what had happened and move on. She had always been very concerned with appearances, twisting virtually everything to fit her own vision of a perfect life and a model family. However, the divorce had turned out to be impossible for even a practiced spin doctor like her to absorb. It had shattered her hopes for that perfect life she'd worked so hard for, and she had all but shut down her former self.

"Lisa!" Mrs. Atwood hurried into the kitchen,

wearing her old chenille bathrobe and carrying a fashion magazine. "Welcome home, dear. How was school today?"

Lisa smiled weakly. She hated seeing that look on her mother's face—that overeager, slightly desperate glitter that meant she was counting on Lisa to make her day worthwhile. "It was okay, Mom," she said, doing her best to sound cheerful and normal. "Nothing special."

"Good, good." Mrs. Atwood tossed her magazine onto the table and clasped her hands in front of her. "Who did you sit with at lunch?"

"Actually, I didn't eat in the cafeteria today," Lisa said as patiently as she could, edging toward the hall. "I went to the library to do some more work on my English paper. Remember? It's due tomorrow."

"Oh, of course!" Mrs. Atwood said. "You told me what it's about. Now, let's see . . ."

"The Canterbury Tales," Lisa supplied. "It's sort of a research report about the Middle Ages." She had told her mother exactly the same thing the day before, but she knew that these days things didn't always sink in at first hearing. "Since it's due tomorrow, I'd better get to work now."

Mrs. Atwood's face fell. "Oh. Of course, dear," she said. "Run along. It's almost time for my favorite talk show anyway."

Lisa couldn't help feeling guilty as she hurried

up the stairs, away from her mother's needy, insistent gaze and voice. She knew that life wasn't easy for her mother. She hadn't had many real friends even before the divorce, and what few there had been had mostly been chased away by her bitterness after Mr. Atwood moved out. In addition, she had found it difficult to find much companionship at work, since her boss was a smarmy, self-important man who was only interested in profit margins and inventory, and most of the other employees were high-school or college students. Aside from Lisa herself, just about the only person Mrs. Atwood spent any time talking to these days was Lisa's aunt Marianne, and she lived in New Jersey, so their conversations were limited by the long-distance phone bill.

Lisa sighed as she dropped her backpack on her tidy white-painted wooden desk and sat down. Her concern for her mother was a familiar feeling by now, but somehow it never got easier to deal with. She did her best to push it out of her mind. She had her own life to worry about, beginning with her English paper . . .

She dug into her backpack, looking for her copy of *The Canterbury Tales*. As she did, her fingers skimmed the stiff fabric of Alex's favorite baseball cap. The passenger-side window of his car had gotten stuck open on their way to the movies on Saturday night, and as he was driving her home, Alex had gallantly insisted on lending her the cap so that her hair wouldn't get tangled by the wind.

She smiled as she remembered the sweet, loving expression in his eyes as he had adjusted the brim over her face. But thinking about that also reminded her of the rest of that evening—particularly the promise she had made to Stevie.

What was I thinking? she wondered as she turned her attention back to her bag. *I never should have promised her I'd tell him. I hadn't even decided yet whether I think he needs to know.*

She bit her lip. Alex hadn't understood her decision to spend the summer in California with her father. How was he going to accept that she had almost decided to stay there permanently? And how could she convince him that considering staying there didn't mean she wasn't in love with him?

Why should I tell him? Why make waves? she thought. *Is it really that important? After all, I did decide to come back, and even the closest couples probably have a few secrets from each other. . . .*

She located her book and pulled it out, setting it on the desk beside her notebook. Then she reached over to flip on her computer. As she waited for it to boot up, she sat back in her chair and thought about how complicated having secrets always made things. Thinking about that reminded her of the other big secret hanging over her head these days—the secret that Max was keeping about Prancer. Lisa had spent half her physics class stewing about her brief conversation with Carole in the hall. What had that expression on Carole's face meant when she'd said, "Sometimes Max has to be the one to make the big decisions?" It had sent an arctic chill down Lisa's spine. Did Carole know—or at least suspect—more than she was telling about Prancer's condition? After all, she spent practically every spare waking hour at the stable. How could she not know what was really going on?

Unless it's something so horrible that Max is even keeping it a secret from Carole, Lisa told herself, her stomach clenching at the very idea. *Maybe Carole's worried about the possibilities, too, and that's why she doesn't want to talk about it.*

At that thought, Lisa couldn't block the list of possible ailments from once again parading through her anxious mind. She had stopped by to visit Prancer every chance she got, so she knew she would have noticed any obvious symptoms or lameness. She also knew the mare couldn't have any serious infectious disease, since Max wouldn't put his other horses at risk by keeping her at the stable. But there were plenty of problems that weren't contagious and didn't have very noticeable external symptoms. Prancer might have leukemia or some other form of cancer. She could be suffering from heart problems, perhaps valvular degeneration. Or, perhaps, some kind of degenerative joint disease. After all, she'd always had that problem with her pedal bone; maybe this was somehow related. She might have a serious gastric ulcer, lymphosarcoma, or even diabetes. For all Lisa knew, Prancer's radial nerve could be paralyzed or her spinal cord might have been injured somehow. Since she hadn't actually seen the horse so much as step out of her stall in weeks, she had no way to judge whether Prancer could still move as well as she always had.

Lisa squeezed her eyes shut and rubbed them hard with both hands, trying to will her pessimistic thoughts away. But it was almost impossible to hold them back—sort of the way it had been impossible for her to look away from those horrible, bloody, stomach-churning films her teacher had shown in driver's ed. She couldn't stand the idea of Prancer—*her* Prancer—suffering from some hopeless, fatal disease. She couldn't stand the thought of Pine Hollow without the sweet, loving mare. But she couldn't stop imagining the worst.

This is ridiculous, Lisa told herself angrily. *If Max realized how nuts this is making me, I'm sure he'd tell me the truth. I've got to talk to him again. And this time I won't let him off the hook until I know what's going on.*

That made her feel better. Whatever was wrong with Prancer, whatever horrible facts she had to face, nothing could be worse than not knowing. She would go to the stable the next day after school, and she wouldn't leave until she was satisfied.

But first she had some work to do, especially if she wanted to make it to Callie's gathering. She glanced at her watch, then turned her attention to her books. This time it was easier to push her worries about Prancer to the back of her mind. Now she knew what she had to do.

Stevie finished gulping down a glass of orange juice and wiped her mouth. "Bye, Michael!" she shouted as she set her empty glass in the sink and headed toward the key rack beside the back door. "You're on your own. I'm out of here!"

Before she could reach for her car keys, she heard footsteps pounding down the stairs. A moment later, her thirteen-year-old brother dashed into the kitchen.

"Wait," he said breathlessly. "Where are you going?"

Stevie gave him an amused look. "Why? Afraid of being left alone?" she teased. "Don't worry, Mommy and Daddy will be home from work in an hour or two. You can hide in the closet until then."

Michael rolled his eyes dramatically. He had started doing that a few months before whenever any of his family members said something he considered stupid. "Very funny, Stevie," he said sarcastically. "You're a laugh riot."

"I try." Stevie turned and fumbled for the horseshoe-shaped key ring that held the keys to the small blue car she shared with Alex. "See ya."

"Wait," Michael said again. This time he took a few steps forward and put a hand on Stevie's arm.

Stevie glanced at him. When he stood this close, she always noticed how tall he was getting. Michael had been shorter than average as a little boy, but a recent growth spurt had brought his height within an inch or so of Stevie's own. Soon, she guessed, he would shoot up until he was as tall as Alex and their oldest brother, Chad. Still, even when that happened Stevie knew she'd always think of him as her little brother. Some things never changed.

"What do you want, squirt?" she asked now. "I've got to go. Phil's expecting me." She had promised to swing by Phil's house and pick him up. Then they were going to drop in on A.J. as they'd planned over the weekend.

"You're going to Phil's?" Michael asked. "Good. Then the mall's right on your way. You can drop me off."

Stevie raised one eyebrow in surprise. "The mall!" she exclaimed with a grin. "Since when do you like to hang out at the mall? I thought you decided it was totally lame after they closed the arcade last year."

Michael rolled his eyes again. "I can decide to go to the mall if I want to," he muttered.

"Sure you can," Stevie agreed cheerfully, still grinning. "You probably want to check out the latest fashions at Sweet Susie's. Or maybe you were planning to get one of those free makeovers at Maxwell's."

Michael's face was turning pink. He shoved his hands in his jeans pockets and backed away. "Never mind," he muttered, sounding angry. "Forget I asked."

Stevie was surprised at his reaction. Like all the Lake kids, Michael had always been able to take teasing as well as he could dish it out. But now he almost looked upset. "What's the matter?" she asked. "I was just kidding. I'll drop you off if you want."

"Forget it." Michael turned away and headed for the refrigerator. "I changed my mind. I don't want to go to the stupid mall anyway."

Stevie shrugged. "Whatever." She didn't have time to figure out her brother's strange mood right then. She was going to have plenty of more important things to think about on the twenty-minute drive to Phil's house—most notably, what in the world the two of them were going to say to A.J. when they saw him.

"Almost there," Scott commented, swerving a bit to avoid a piece of debris on the highway. "Last chance to change your mind and turn back. If we ignore the fact that she's here, maybe she'll go away."

"Very funny," Callie muttered, playing nervously with the buckle of her seat belt. She and Scott were on their way to pick up Sheila. Callie had begun the trip hopefully, but the closer they got to the airport, the more anxious she felt. And the obnoxious comments Scott had been making about Sheila weren't helping her mood.

She glanced into the side mirror, checking that her blond hair was behaving and that everything else was in order. Once again, she noticed the way the blue shirt she had chosen to wear set off her dark blue eyes.

Of course, that was no accident, she accused herself silently. *You know very well that Sheila has always wished she had blue eyes. Very mature, Callie. You're off to a great start with this bold new friendship stuff.*

She averted her eyes from her reflection. Why was she so nervous, anyway? This was Sheila she was talking about—the girl she had made mud pies with when they were both still in diapers, the girl who had known her when she had braces, the girl she had told about her very first kiss . . .

Chill! she told herself sternly. *This really shouldn't be a big deal, so don't turn it into one. All you're trying to do here is trust a little more, to stop competing and start sharing. That shouldn't be so hard. Not with Sheila.*

She sighed. It *was* going to be hard, and she knew it. That had nothing to do with Sheila, and everything to do with Callie herself.

"Callie!" Sheila squealed, hurrying forward with her arms outspread. "You look fabulous!"

Callie automatically returned her friend's hug. "Yeah, right," she said dryly. "The metal look is totally in, here on the East Coast."

Sheila pulled back and glanced at Callie's crutches. "Don't be silly," she insisted, pushing back her thick, wavy, dark brown hair. "I almost didn't notice those. You look great, you really do."

"So do you." Callie was feeling a bit over-whelmed. She and Scott had arrived in the terminal moments before to find that Sheila's plane had landed early and that Sheila was already waiting for them. Callie hadn't had any time to prepare herself for their reunion, and now here it was, suddenly upon her.

She looked her friend over. Sheila really did look fantastic. Her hair had grown since Callie had seen her last, and now it tumbled over her shoulders. Her face was tanned and healthy-looking, and her clothes looked as neat and crisp as always, despite the fact that she had just spent several hours on a plane en route from a round of interviews in Boston.

Meanwhile, Sheila had turned her attention to Scott. "My, my," she said with a throaty, flirtatious laugh. "I'd almost forgotten how handsome you are, Cookie."

Callie hid a smile. Scott was doing his best not to show it as he gave Sheila the briefest of hugs, but she could tell he was already annoyed. He had always hated the nickname Cookie, which was why Sheila had always used it.

"Let's go pick up your luggage, Sheila," Scott suggested. "Then maybe we can beat the rush hour out of here."

Sheila turned to Callie as Scott headed toward the baggage area. "Are you okay?" she asked, looking worried. "Do you need any help with those?"

Callie gritted her teeth. *She's just trying to be helpful,* she thought. *Don't look for trouble.* She knew she could sometimes be too sensitive, and she didn't want to ruin things before they got started.

"I'm fine," she said, doing her best to sound

normal. "I've had plenty of practice with these crutches lately. I'm practically an expert."

"That's great." Sheila glanced around the airport and groaned dramatically as the two girls moved along after Scott. "I'll tell you something, Callie, I'm really getting sick of airports. This trip has been perfectly exhausting."

"How have the interviews been going?" Callie asked, careful not to allow herself to sound breathless. Sheila was walking a little faster than Callie was used to, and she was having to work hard to keep up on her crutches without seeming to hurry.

Sheila waved one hand dismissively. "Oh, you know," she said lazily. "They're all kind of the same, really. All the schools just want to hear about my grades, my test scores, my academic prizes, that sort of thing. I really don't know why these interviews are even necessary; everything they need to know is on my transcript." She glanced at Callie and smiled. "But enough of that boring business. Tell me what you've been up to lately. How's your new school?"

"Great." Callie hesitated, not quite knowing how to describe her first weeks at Fenton Hall. Should she start off by raving about the wonderful academic reputation of the school and the advanced degrees held by many of the teachers?

Or should she reveal how nervous she had been, stepping into a world where most of the students had known each other since kindergarten?

She could guess what Stevie's answer to that question would be. But somehow she didn't feel quite ready yet to open up. Not here, in public, so soon . . .

"It's been okay," she said cautiously, opting for a compromise. "You know, starting a new school is always kind of tough."

Sheila nodded. "Oh, I know!" she exclaimed. "It must be so awful. Especially after . . . well, you know." She glanced once more at Callie's crutches. "I mean, your accident even made the news back home. It must have been kind of embarrassing to start school after all that publicity."

"Right," Callie said weakly. This was even harder than she had expected. Everything Sheila said—no matter how innocent, how sympathetic—was rubbing her the wrong way. She cleared her throat. "Of course, at a school like Fenton Hall, the people aren't nearly as immature as most of the kids back home. So that made things a lot easier for me."

Sheila didn't seem to have a ready answer for that, and Callie felt a moment of triumph. But her elation almost immediately turned to sadness. What was wrong with her, anyway? She knew she wanted to improve her relationship with Sheila. But how could she if she couldn't even change her own behavior?

SIX

"Come in, come in!" Mrs. McDonnell swung the door wide open and beamed. "It's wonderful to see you. Stevie, it's been too long."

"Hello, Mrs. McDonnell," Stevie said politely, stepping inside.

Phil followed her. "Who's that hiding behind the banister?" he called out playfully.

Stevie heard a giggle. Glancing in the direction Phil was looking, she saw A.J.'s six-year-old sister, Elizabeth, clinging to the stair rails and smiling shyly at them.

"Hi, Elizabeth," Stevie said, waggling her fingers at the little girl. "Remember me? I'm A.J.'s friend Stevie."

Elizabeth's smile faded, and her round face became solemn. "A.J. doesn't have any friends," she said, so softly that for a moment Stevie wasn't sure she'd heard her right. "He doesn't like anybody anymore. Not even me."

Mrs. McDonnell's face paled, and she hurried

97

over to the little girl. "That's not true, Lizzie," she said gently, kneeling down and putting her hands on her daughter's shoulders. "Daddy and I talked to you about this, remember?"

The little girl nodded, but Stevie thought her eyes still looked sad. *Poor kid,* she thought. *She probably has no idea what happened to the nice, friendly big brother she used to have. And how could she? None of the rest of us understands it, either.*

Mrs. McDonnell had risen to her feet again and was gazing at Phil hopefully. "I'm so glad you decided to come by today," she said, her voice choked with worry. "If anyone can reach him . . ." She rubbed her forehead. "Well, I just don't know what else to do anymore. My husband and I are at our wits' end. We feel as though our wonderful son has been taken away from us and there's a—a stranger here now in his place."

"Don't worry," Stevie said as cheerfully as she could. "I'm sure Phil and I can smack some sense into him."

"I hope so." But the woman didn't look very optimistic.

Phil glanced at the stairs. "Do you mind if we head straight up?" he asked. "Is he in his room?"

"All the time now," Mrs. McDonnell replied with a touch of bitterness. "Go on up. And good luck."

Stevie let Phil lead the way upstairs. She had

been in the McDonnells' house before, but only downstairs. Much like the first story, the second story of the spacious colonial home was casual and comfortable, with cheerful throw rugs on the polished pine floors and family photographs decorating nearly every spare bit of wall space.

Phil headed for a closed door about halfway down the upstairs hall. Stevie could hear rock music pounding away from the room on the other side.

"Here we go," Phil murmured. Taking a deep breath, he knocked on the door.

"What?" came a voice from within.

Stevie felt an unpleasant jolt of surprise. If she hadn't known better, she would have thought a stranger had answered Phil's knock. That morose, sullen voice couldn't belong to A.J., could it?

Phil didn't bother to answer. He simply swung the door open and stepped inside, a brave smile on his face. "Surprise," he said. "Stevie and I were in the neighborhood, so we decided to stop by and say hello."

Stevie entered the room after Phil. The first thing that met her eyes was A.J., lying on his unmade bed and staring up at the ceiling. Both stereo speakers, positioned on a dresser nearby, were aimed directly at his head. The music was a lot louder in there, and Phil had to raise his voice to be heard.

"So how are you doing, buddy?" he went on, taking a step toward the bed.

A.J. had raised his head off the mattress when Phil first spoke. Now he let it fall back heavily and returned his gaze to the ceiling. "Okay," he said dully. "What do you guys want?"

Stevie raised one eyebrow in surprise. "Do we need a reason to stop by and hang out?" she asked, purposely keeping her voice light and playful.

A.J. didn't bother to answer. He tapped his fingers against the bed frame in time to the pounding music.

Phil glanced at Stevie, worry in his deep green eyes. But when he spoke, his voice was as carefully cheerful as Stevie's had been. "So what's up with you these days, man?" he asked, taking a step closer to the bed. "You're turning into quite the hermit lately."

"Right," Stevie added, forcing a laugh. "If we didn't have such big egos, we'd think you stopped liking us or something."

A.J. propped his head up on one hand and looked at them. His face remained passive. "I don't know what you mean," he said dully.

Stevie shoved her hands in her jeans pockets to stop them from shaking. This was really weird. She had known that A.J. wasn't acting like himself these days—Phil had told her that often enough—but she hadn't been expecting anything like this. Who was this cold, distant stranger lying on the bed in front of them? He looked like A.J., he even sounded a little like A.J., but he wasn't acting like A.J. at all.

"Hey, dude, if we have B.O. or something, you can tell us, you know," Phil returned. "We won't . . ." His voice trailed off, and he gulped.

Glancing over at him quickly, Stevie guessed what was happening. He had been trying, as she had, to joke around with A.J. in the way he always had, hoping to tease him into telling them what was bothering him. But that clearly wasn't working, and now Phil was too worried to go on. Stevie reached over and squeezed his hand.

"Listen, A.J.," she said bluntly. "You're acting like a totally different person or something. We want to know why."

Phil cleared his throat. "You really haven't been acting like yourself, man," he went on, his voice serious now. "We're worried about you. I know you're bummed about the Julianna thing, but—"

"This has nothing to do with Julianna," A.J. interrupted sharply. He rolled over on his side, reaching for the volume control on the CD player. Giving it a sharp twist, he raised the volume another few decibels.

Stevie winced. The music was so loud now that they would have to shout to be heard. *What's his problem?* she thought with a flash of irritation. *We're trying to help, and he's being a total jerk.*

Phil scowled. Taking a few steps forward, he grabbed the volume knob and twisted it back the other way until the music was barely a whisper.

"Hey!" A.J. protested angrily, reaching for the knob again.

Phil grabbed his wrist and held it. "Listen, man," he said angrily. "This has gone far enough."

Stevie reacted quickly. Phil was an easygoing guy most of the time, but he had clearly reached his boiling point. "You're right about that," she said, grabbing her boyfriend by the arm. "Let go. I think it's time for us to get out of here."

Phil shot her a furious glance. But after a second he released his grip on A.J.'s arm. "Fine," he said, his jaw clenched tightly. "There doesn't seem to be much point in staying."

Stevie sighed in relief and glanced at A.J., who was sitting up now, rubbing his wrist and frowning. He was significantly shorter and slighter than Phil, which was sometimes easy to forget since his personality tended to fill any room he was in. But now Stevie couldn't help noticing how pale and thin A.J. looked, how much smaller he really was than the more athletically built Phil. Then again, she had never seen the two friends come so close to a physical confrontation before.

She put an arm around Phil's waist. "Come on," she said as calmly as she could manage. "Let's go." Her own anger at A.J. had fled in the face of Phil's sudden outburst, and all she could think about was getting out of there before things got out of hand. They would go back to Phil's house, talk this over, see what they could come up with. Stevie usually wasn't one to back down from a fight, but in this case she suspected that if she and Phil lost their tempers with A.J., things would only get worse. They had to figure out a different way to help him.

Phil gave A.J. one last angry glare, but he allowed Stevie to steer him out of the room. Stevie glanced over her shoulder as she pulled the bedroom door shut behind her. She was just in time to see A.J. shrug, then turn to the CD player to crank up the volume once more. The throbbing beat of the music followed them as they made their way out of the house.

"Tell me, Sheila," Congressman Forester said, reaching for the salad bowl in the middle of the dining room table, "are you enjoying the college interview process?"

Callie poked listlessly at her food with her fork. Her parents had commandeered Sheila's attention from the moment she had stepped into the house an hour before, bombarding her with questions about people and events back home. Scott had been uncharacteristically quiet on the ride home from the airport, and he was maintaining his silence now as the family ate dinner.

"This is such a thrilling time of your life, isn't it, Sheila?" Mrs. Forester chimed in before Sheila could respond. "You and Callie are getting so grown up—looking at colleges and all that sort of thing!"

"I guess that's true," Sheila replied. "It would be fun if Callie and I were doing this interview thing together." She glanced over at Callie with a half smile. "But I guess she's too attached to high school to let it go quite yet. And, of course, she is younger than me."

Mr. and Mrs. Forester chuckled, Scott rolled his eyes, and Callie smiled tightly, pretending to be too involved with her rice to answer. Shoving a forkful into her mouth, she chewed slowly as the others turned their attention to a discussion of Sheila's interviews in Virginia, D.C., and Pennsylvania.

How did I do this before? Callie wondered helplessly. *Have I really changed that much in a few short months?*

She suspected she had, and the thought made her uncomfortable. Six months ago, shooting back some dry, witty response to Sheila's comment would have come as naturally to her as breathing. But now that she was trying to make a change, she didn't know what to say, how to act, or even how to feel.

I really do want to change things between us, she thought, glancing at Sheila out of the corner of her eye. *I want to be a better person, a better friend to her, than I was before. I'm just not sure how to do that.*

Somehow, once she and Sheila were together again, all Stevie's clear, logical advice had flown right out of her mind. All Callie could seem to do was react in her usual ways to Sheila's usual comments. She'd been holding back as much as possible, staying quiet and letting things pass, but she couldn't seem to take that next step and move their conversations in a different direction.

Meanwhile, her parents were still chatting with Sheila about her college tour. "How are the athletics programs at the schools you've visited so far?" Congressman Forester asked. "I remember how much you always loved playing volleyball, Sheila. Are you still on the Valley Vista High varsity team?"

"I never tried out for varsity," Sheila replied with a mild, self-satisfied smile. "I considered it, but I knew it would be a major time commitment and I didn't want to spread myself too thin. You know, what with student government, the school paper, the select chorale, yearbook, honor society

105

meetings—all that stuff was already taking up so much time, I didn't think it was a good idea to take on another activity."

Not to mention the fact that all through sophomore year the JV coach kept threatening to cut you if you tripped over your big clumsy feet one more time. The catty comment formed itself automatically in her mind. Callie opened her mouth to deliver it with her most practiced ironic tone, ready to cut Sheila back down to size.

But she stopped herself just in time, smiling blandly instead. *I do want to change,* she thought a bit desperately. *I really do. But how can I when everything in me wants to prove myself to Sheila, just like always?*

Somehow Callie survived through the rest of dinner. For once she was actually grateful that both her parents loved to talk so much, since they kept Sheila busy trading gossip and news. As she rose to help clear the table, Callie checked her watch.

Good, she thought with relief. *The others should be here soon.*

As if on cue, the doorbell chimed.

"I'll get it," Callie said quickly. She glanced at Sheila. "It's probably those friends I told you about. Like I said, I invited them to stop by after dinner."

Sheila nodded agreeably. "Sounds like fun."

Mrs. Forester smiled. "Oh, Sheila, they're marvelous people," she said. "I'm sure you'll really like them. Why don't you two girls run along and show everyone into the family room? I'll be in in a moment with a little dessert or something for all of you, all right?"

"Thanks, Mom." Callie knew that the "little dessert or something" was sure to turn out to be one of her mother's usual understated yet impressive spreads, the kind of casually elegant party food that most people had catered but that Mrs. Forester could whip up herself on the spur of the moment.

Leaving Scott to help clear the table, Callie hurried to the front hall. Sheila followed. "I can't wait to see who you've been hanging with out here, Callie," Sheila commented with a laugh. "Every time I try to imagine what the kids in Virginia must be like, I keep picturing the people on that old TV show, *Hee Haw*. I know they're not really anything like that—are they?"

"See for yourself." Callie swung open the door and found Stevie, Phil, and Alex standing on the other side. She stood back to let them enter. "Hi, guys," she said. "Come on in and meet Sheila."

Sheila was standing back a little. As Callie turned, she saw her friend discreetly sizing up the newcomers.

"This is Phil Marsten," Callie said politely. "Phil, my friend from back home, Sheila. And this is Alex Lake. Alex, meet Sheila."

Sheila shook hands with the two boys, smiling approvingly. Callie wasn't surprised. Phil and Alex were right up Sheila's alley. She liked her guys tall, broad-shouldered, and cute, and both of these guys fit that bill.

Meanwhile, Stevie stepped forward. "Hi," she said in her usual straightforward way. "I'm Alex's sister, Stevie." She stuck out her hand. "I don't usually admit that he and I are related," she joked, "but since you're Callie's friend . . ."

Sheila took Stevie's hand and chuckled politely, but this time her smile seemed the slightest bit frosty, at least to Callie's practiced eye. Suddenly seeing Stevie as Sheila must've seen her—her well-worn blue jeans coming apart at the knees, her sneakers with the ratty laces and a hole in one toe, her faded Pine Hollow T-shirt with an old denim shirt over it—Callie cringed with embarrassment. Why did Stevie always have to dress like some kind of refugee? Couldn't she wear something decent for an occasion like this? It wasn't as though her lawyer parents couldn't afford to buy her decent clothes. After all, Alex looked perfectly presentable in khakis and a polo shirt.

Just then Stevie turned to Callie. "Have you heard from Lisa?" she asked. "I know she was really worried about her paper. I hope it's going okay." She turned to Sheila. "Our friend Lisa is totally brilliant," she explained proudly, "but she doesn't even realize it, especially when she's in the middle of a tough assignment."

At Stevie's words, Callie felt a rush of shame sweep over her. She hadn't even remembered that Lisa was working on her English paper that afternoon, but naturally Stevie had. Stevie was a good friend. *I shouldn't be so critical about stupid stuff like clothes,* she thought, feeling angry with herself. *No wonder I'm having trouble relating to Sheila. I can't expect her to share all her innermost thoughts and feelings if I'm always sizing her up, looking for weaknesses. What kind of shallow, stuck-up person am I, anyway?* She frowned at herself. *I'm surprised Stevie and the others even put up with me.*

Doing her best to hide her tumultuous thoughts, Callie led the others into the large, comfortable family room to their left. Unlike the more formal living room across the hall, the family room was decorated in bright, cheerful colors and cozy furnishings. One wall was dominated by a huge, brick-fronted fireplace, and another by an entertainment system complete with television, VCR, and stereo.

Stevie, as usual, made herself at home right away. Flopping down on the couch, she glanced at her watch. "I was afraid we were going to be late," she told Callie. "Phil and I were right on schedule, of course, but when we stopped by my house to pick up Alex, he was still eating."

Alex rolled his eyes. "How was your flight, Sheila?" he asked, pointedly ignoring his sister. "Callie told us you were flying in from Boston."

As Sheila perched on the hearth and started chatting with Alex and Phil, Callie went over and sat down beside Stevie. She was already feeling a little better now that the informal party had started. Callie wasn't usually a party person—she preferred dealing with people one on one. But in this case, she felt she needed some support from her new friends. Callie wasn't afraid of a challenge. If she were, she wouldn't have taken up a sport like endurance riding. She had competed in races where only her iron will kept her going over rough terrain, through terrible weather. Once she had ridden the last six miles of a fifty-mile race in pouring rain, on a course she had never ridden before, with a broken shoelace and a badly bruised kneecap. Her recuperation after the accident was another example of how far she could go on sheer determination. Instead of giving in to despair when she learned the extent of the damage done to her body, Callie had taken her doctors' diagnosis as a challenge, forcing her unresponsive muscles to relearn their tasks as quickly as possible in her quest to regain full strength and mobility.

But changing her relationship with Sheila was different. For one thing, it already seemed much more difficult and confusing than anything she had faced before. Callie wasn't certain where this challenge would lead her. The rewards were there, to be sure, but they weren't as clear or as easy to grasp as a golden endurance trophy or a brisk walk across a room without leaning on her crutches. What did she want from her oldest friend, anyway? She needed her new friends to remind her by example.

At that moment Mrs. Forester walked in, bearing a tray loaded with cookies and brownies. Scott was behind her with a large pitcher of lemonade. "Dig in," Mrs. Forester sang out, expertly arranging napkins, glasses, and treats on the wide wooden coffee table.

"Gladly." Stevie eagerly reached for the largest brownie on the platter. "Yum! Good thing Emily's not here yet," she said with a grin. "She loves your walnut brownies even more than I do, Mrs. Forester."

Mrs. Forester smiled and thanked Stevie, then graciously excused herself and disappeared, leaving the kids alone once again. "Emily?" Callie repeated slowly. She gulped, running over the past few days in her memory. "Um, did you mention to her that we'd be getting together tonight? I think I forgot to tell her about it the other day."

"I don't think so," Stevie replied, taking another large bite of her brownie.

Callie bit her lip. "Oops. I guess I messed up."

Stevie merely shrugged and leaned over to accept the glass of lemonade that Phil had just poured for her. But Callie felt horrible about the mix-up. How could she have forgotten to invite Emily? Had it really been an innocent oversight? Or had she neglected to invite Emily because subconsciously she knew Emily wasn't the kind of friend who was likely to impress Sheila? Emily was a wonderful person, but most people tended to notice her crutches and her stiff, clumsy walk long before they noticed her brilliant smile or her offbeat sense of humor. Besides that, Emily had a direct, candid, almost childlike quality that sometimes made her seem much more different from the average sixteen-year-old than her cerebral palsy did. Somehow, Callie couldn't imagine how Sheila would react to Emily. Would she see her for the wonderful, special person she was, the person who was helping Callie more than anyone else to gain the strength to walk again? Or would she see her as a weird handicapped kid who talked too much?

Callie wondered if she was being unfair to Sheila. She couldn't help remembering too many times in the past when the two of them had made fun of people who were different—too fat, too skinny, poorly dressed, or just not quite cool enough. But most of that had been years ago, when they were just kids who didn't know any better. They were both older now, more mature. Besides, if Callie was going to be honest with herself, she had to admit that she had started that childhood teasing at least as often as Sheila had. If she had become a more open-minded person as she got older and wiser, surely Sheila had, too.

As Callie struggled with her thoughts, Stevie was chewing her brownie slowly and watching Sheila talk to Alex. The two of them were still sitting near the fireplace, chatting and laughing together.

So this is Sheila, Stevie mused, doing her best to observe the other girl without seeming to stare. Luckily, Phil and Scott were standing nearby having one of their interminable conversations about football, so Stevie could pretend to listen to them while actually concentrating on Sheila.

So far, she wasn't quite sure what to think of Callie's friend. Stevie tended to size people up pretty quickly, but she wasn't especially critical of them at first meeting. She tended to look for people's good qualities first and try to like them. Unless someone was a total snob or a real jerk, she preferred to give them the benefit of the doubt, to judge them likable until proven unlikable.

Sheila certainly didn't seem snobby in the way

Veronica diAngelo and her clique were, and so far she had been perfectly nice to Stevie and the others. But Stevie still found herself uncertain what to think. There was something about the way Sheila looked at people—something a little too observant, maybe?

Then again, Stevie had to admit that maybe she was just looking for an excuse not to like Sheila because of the way she had latched on to her twin. Stevie's eyes narrowed slightly as Sheila put her hand on Alex's arm and leaned forward to whisper something to him. Alex grinned in response, and Sheila shook back her thick dark hair and let out a throaty giggle. Stevie couldn't hear what they were talking about, but she didn't really care. The only thing she cared about was that Sheila was flirting with her brother in a big way, and Alex didn't even seem to mind.

To be fair, I guess Sheila has no way of knowing that Alex is spoken for. And he's so clueless about this stuff that it would probably never occur to him that she's flirting her head off, let alone that he should realize it might be a good idea to mention Lisa's name, Stevie thought. *Still, I wish Lisa would hurry up and get here already and put a stop to this.*

She hardly heard the phone ringing in the other room, but a moment later Mrs. Forester stuck her head in. "Sorry to interrupt, kids," she said. "Just wanted to let you know that Lisa just called."

"What did she say?" Callie asked. "Is she coming?"

"Such a lovely, polite girl," Mrs. Forester said. "She was just calling to apologize for being late and explain that she's finishing up her homework. She'll be here in a little while."

"Great!" Stevie exclaimed with a grin. "That's great."

Mrs. Forester looked amused. "My my, Stevie. If I didn't know better I'd think you were the one dating Lisa instead of Alex."

Stevie grinned weakly as the others laughed, but secretly she was thanking Mrs. Forester for the comment. *There's no way Sheila could have missed that one,* she thought, sneaking a glance at the dark-haired girl. Sure enough, Sheila had a slight frown on her face. She stood and walked toward the coffee table, where she helped herself to a cookie and then looked around, as if seeking someone new to talk to.

Stevie breathed a sigh of relief. "So, Sheila," she said, suddenly feeling much friendlier toward the visitor. She patted the sofa cushion beside her. "Why don't you have a seat? I'm sure you must have some good stories about what Callie was like as a little girl."

Stevie was still chatting with Sheila when Lisa arrived twenty minutes later, breathless and full of

115

apologies. "It was my paper," Lisa explained to Callie. "I just couldn't get the last paragraph right. I must have rewritten it twenty times."

"No problem." Callie handed Lisa a glass of lemonade. "You're not even the last one here. Carole hasn't showed up yet."

Stevie frowned, realizing it was true. She glanced at her watch. Where was Carole, anyway?

Lisa looked surprised, too. "Maybe she forgot it was tonight," she said uncertainly. "You know how she can be."

That's probably it, Stevie decided. Carole was flaking out again, working late at the stable. She had probably lost track of time as usual, more concerned with making sure every strand of Starlight's mane was lying smoothly than with the plans she had made. Stevie rolled her eyes at the thought.

As Callie pulled Sheila away to introduce her to Lisa, Stevie leaned back against the sofa cushions. After talking with Sheila for a while, Stevie still wasn't sure what she thought of her, but she was doing her best to keep an open mind. All that really mattered was what Callie thought. Regardless of her own opinion about Sheila, Stevie still wanted Callie to learn to open up more with her closest and oldest friend.

Best friends should trust each other, she told herself. *That's the way things work.* Unbidden, an image of Phil angrily grabbing A.J.'s arm popped into her mind. *The way they should work, anyway.* She was still having trouble reconciling the new A.J., the brooding, silent, sullen A.J. who lay on his bed and stared at nothing, with the likable, fun-loving A.J. she had known for so many years.

She was still turning that one over in her mind a few minutes later when Carole finally walked into the room. She was dressed in one of her typical stable outfits—worn jodhpurs and a T-shirt.

"Hey!" Scott called. "You made it. We were starting to think you got lost in the hayloft or something."

Carole looked surprised. "What do you mean?"

"Never mind." Callie gave her brother a chastising glance. "We're just glad you're here. Help yourself to some cookies. If you just came from the stable, you must be starving."

"Thanks, Callie." Carole wandered toward the coffee table and perched on the edge of the couch beside Stevie. She reached for a butterscotch brownie.

"Come on, Carole," Stevie said teasingly. "You can tell me the truth. Did you lose track of time because Starlight slobbered on your watch while you were hugging him and murmuring sweet nothings in his ear? Or did you just get distracted trying to figure out which horse in the stable has the prettiest mane?"

Carole glanced at her, looking slightly annoyed. "Very funny, Stevie," she said. "If you must know, I was with Samson. I can't blow off his training just to rush over to hang out with you guys, you know."

Now it was Stevie's turn to be surprised. Carole's words had been uncharacteristically testy. Besides that, she was almost an hour late. Carole could be flaky about getting places on time, but she was usually perfectly willing to admit it.

"Whatever," she said. "I was just kidding. We were kind of worried when you didn't show up for so long."

Carole shrugged. "Sorry. I guess I'm kind of tired."

Stevie nodded absently. Her thoughts were already drifting away from Carole, back to her encounter with A.J. It had given her a weird, scary feeling to see him in his room earlier. It had almost seemed as if she were looking at a totally different person. How could someone—someone she thought she knew almost as well as she knew Phil himself—change overnight like that? What could have happened? What could he be hiding from even his best, most caring friends?

She sighed. She was starting to see why Carole and Ben Marlow and others like them sometimes seemed to prefer horses to people. Sometimes horses were easier to figure out.

If a horse is sick, it shows it through its symptoms, Stevie thought. *If a horse is scared, it lets you know in no uncertain terms. If a horse has serious problems—faults in conformation, broken wind, stable vices, whatever—you can figure out what's wrong just by looking, maybe calling the vet. It's different with people. All our worst conformation faults are inside, where others only see if we let them.* She shook her head grimly, remembering the dull, hopeless look in A.J.'s eyes. *And when we start keeping the bad stuff a secret, even our friends can't help us.*

SEVEN

"Group two, that's enough. Rest time," the phys ed teacher barked. "Group three, you're up."

Stevie jogged toward the gym bleachers with the rest of group two. She flopped down dramatically on the lowest bleacher beside Callie. "Finally," she panted. "I thought she was never going to let us stop doing those push-ups."

Callie laughed. "Almost makes me glad I get to sit out gym class this term," she said. "I forgot how horrible these state fitness tests can be."

"Tell me about it." Stevie wiped her brow and glanced out at the members of group three, who were lowering themselves to the red and blue synthetic mats that lined the floor in the center of the gym. Her gaze wandered to the closest mat, where Veronica diAngelo was holding court with several of her friends. Group three was supposed to be warming up in preparation for its fitness tests, but to Stevie, Veronica's stretches looked more like the

120

kind one might do when first waking up after a long, restful night's sleep.

Callie followed her gaze. "Is it just me, or does she always have that queen-of-the-world look about her?"

"More like queen of the dorks," Stevie replied, rolling her eyes. She had known Veronica a long time, and they had never gotten along. Back in junior high, Veronica had been a regular riding student at Pine Hollow along with Stevie and her friends. But even then Veronica had cared more about her fancy riding clothes' designer labels and her purebred horses' designer bloodlines than she had about actually learning anything about riding. A couple of years later, Veronica had finally grown bored with horses and traded her time at the stable for more time at the mall prowling for guys. Nobody at Pine Hollow missed her much, least of all Stevie.

Stevie turned away from Veronica and her friends, giving her full attention to Callie. "Sorry we didn't get much chance to talk last night," she said. "It was great to meet Sheila, though. I think everyone really liked her."

Even as she said it, Stevie had to admit to herself that it was a sizable white lie. She still wasn't sure she liked Sheila much at all. Lisa had seemed really distracted—probably by worries over her paper, or maybe her paranoia about Prancer—and had spent most of the evening smiling politely at everything anyone else said. After her late arrival, Carole had only stayed for about half an hour before making an excuse about doing laundry and taking off.

"I just wish I'd remembered to invite Emily," Callie said. "And I wish A.J. had come."

"Fat chance," Stevie said. "I saw the new A.J. for myself yesterday, and believe me, he didn't look to be in a partying mood."

Callie smiled sympathetically. "I know. Phil told me a little bit about that last night," she said. "Do you want to talk about it?"

Stevie waved one hand wearily. She had spent a lot of time since the previous afternoon thinking about A.J., and so far she hadn't come up with any useful revelations. "Not really," she told Callie. "Anyway, A.J. has been a weirdo for weeks now. Sheila's only here for a couple more days. I'd rather talk about her. So how are things going?"

"I don't know." Callie kicked absently at the metal support of the bleacher with her good leg. "We went straight to bed after you guys left last night, and this morning my dad talked her ear off about that new welfare committee he's on in Congress. So I feel like we haven't talked much yet."

"You still have time," Stevie assured her. "Where is she today? I thought maybe she'd come to school with you."

"Nope. She's touring a couple of local colleges today. Including Northern Virginia U., by the way. Isn't that where your older brother goes?"

"Yeah, but she shouldn't let that stop her from going there," Stevie said. "With any luck Chad will have flunked out long before next fall." She was kidding—her oldest brother, Chad, was doing very well at the university. "Seriously, it's an awesome school. What's she planning to major in?"

"I'm not sure," Callie replied. "She likes history, and she's always been interested in writing—you know, newspaper and yearbook stuff."

"Well, NVU's supposed to have a great journalism department." Stevie grinned. "I only know that because the last time Chad called home, he was totally gaga over some girl he met who's a journalism major."

Callie grinned back. She had heard plenty of stories over the past months about Chad's legendary romantic life. It sounded as though he had spent the past five or six years of his life falling for a new girl every week.

Her smile faded as her thoughts returned to Sheila. She would be back from her tours by the time Callie got home from school, and Callie was already dreading seeing her again. Her gaze was trained on her classmates out on the mats, who were beginning their first set of push-ups, but she wasn't really seeing them. Instead she was seeing

123

Sheila as she had first seen her at the airport the afternoon before, perfectly groomed and staring sympathetically at her crutches.

"It's weird," she said softly, after looking around to make sure none of the other students was close enough to hear. "I've known Sheila my whole life. But now it's like I'm not sure what to say to her."

Stevie shrugged. "I know it must be tough. But just try to say what you're really feeling instead of what you think she wants to hear, and things should work out all right."

Callie ran her fingers lightly over the top support of one of her crutches. Stevie made it all sound so simple. And for someone like her, it probably was simple. Stevie never seemed to worry about what other people thought of her. She just went ahead and did and said what she wanted and things worked out for her somehow. Callie wished she could be like that, but she didn't think it was likely to happen. The best she could hope for was to learn to be a little less guarded, a little more trusting, with a few select people in her life.

Her thoughts were suddenly interrupted by a shriek from the gym floor. Callie glanced over and saw Veronica leaping to her feet.

"Ow!" Veronica squealed. "Ow, ow, ow!"

"What's the matter?" the phys ed teacher asked, rushing toward her.

Veronica gave the teacher a sour look. "I have a cramp in my leg," she whined. "I should have known it was too soon to start exercising again after that terrible flu I had last week."

Stevie smirked and leaned toward Callie. "Right," she whispered sarcastically. "It's the dreaded Bermuda flu. It managed to keep her out of commission straight through a four-day weekend."

The teacher made a few soothing noises, then sent Veronica over to sit in the bleachers. "Over here, Veronica!" someone called from a few rows behind Stevie and Callie. "Come sit with us."

Veronica headed for the voice. As she stepped onto the bleacher seat beside Callie, the edge of her white leather sneaker hit one of Callie's crutches, sending it clattering to the floor.

Callie winced at the noise, which momentarily silenced the students all around them, and automatically bent over to retrieve the crutch, grimacing at the movement, which strained her weakened right side.

"Hey, watch where you're putting your big feet, Veronica," Stevie said. She leaned over and helped Callie grab the crutch.

"Why don't you tell your little friend to watch herself, Stevie?" Veronica demanded. "It's bad enough she sits around here every class and watches the rest of us sweat. The least she could do is keep her stupid stuff out of the way." With a toss of her dark hair, Veronica moved on without a backward glance.

"What a jerk," Stevie muttered. She glanced at Callie. "Sorry about that."

Callie bit her lip and shrugged. "Not your fault," she said, trying not to let Stevie see how much Veronica's casual insult had bothered her. She hated being this way—hated standing out from the crowd because of her injuries, hated sitting on the sidelines during class, most of all hated relying on those ugly metal crutches. It was one thing to be different because of an achievement or talent, like when she won an endurance race or received an academic award. But this difference was more like the extra attention she and Scott got because of their father's job. She hadn't asked for it, she hadn't done anything to earn or deserve it, she didn't want it. But it was there, and she had to deal with it every day of her life, like it or not.

She sighed and pushed the crutches a few inches away on the wooden seat, reminding herself that this was temporary. In a few weeks or months she wouldn't need the crutches anymore, and people like Veronica diAngelo could go back to ignoring her. If only that day didn't feel so far in the future . . . In a way, she mused, her life since the accident had been a little like an endurance ride. At the beginning her ultimate recovery had seemed impossibly far away, like the finish line in a hundred-mile race. Now that she was more than halfway there, there still seemed much too far to go, too many miles left for her weary mind to imagine.

But if it really is like a race, it will all be worth it in the end, Callie reminded herself, feeling her old determination taking over once again. *The day I can finally throw these stupid crutches out in the garbage will be better than crossing a thousand finish lines. I just have to dig in and hold on until then.*

Carole chewed on her lower lip, her eyes trained on Ms. Shepard. The teacher was shuffling some papers on her desk as a few stragglers wandered into the classroom.

The bell went off with a jangling buzz, and Carole jumped nervously in her seat. She gripped the edges of her desk, wishing for the magical ability to move time forward by will alone. Just five minutes, maybe ten—that would be enough. Then she would already know the truth, for better or for worse. She would have yesterday's test paper sitting in front of her. As it was, she feared the suspense might overwhelm her before the teacher got around to passing out the grades.

"Every Pine Hollow student must maintain a C

average or above." Max's words floated through her mind before she could stop them. *"Any student whose average falls below that level in any subject will not be allowed to ride until he or she brings up the grade."*

Max said the same thing every year, gave the same warning to every new crop of Pine Hollow students. Carole had heard him say it as part of his introductory speech to the beginners' riding class just a few weeks before. At the time the words had hardly registered, they were so familiar from years of repetition. But now they seemed burned into her brain, throbbing there, taunting her with their black-and-white, unmistakable meaning.

It's not going to happen, she told herself, crossing her fingers hopefully. *I answered most of the questions. Maybe I got lucky. Maybe this was a practice test or something. Or graded on a really easy curve.*

"All right, class," Ms. Shepard called. "Settle down. I'm going to pass out your tests now. Most of you did fairly well."

Carole bit her lip so hard that it started to go numb. The teacher dropped a couple of papers on nearby desks, then glanced down at the next test in the pile.

"Carole," Ms. Shepard said, turning toward her. She fingered the corner of the paper. "Carole, I must say I'm a little surprised at your performance. I'd like you to stay after class so we can talk about it."

Before Carole had a chance to digest that, her test paper landed on her desk. The grade, written in bold red ink in the top right-hand corner, hit her like a sledgehammer between the eyes.

F.

Carole felt her hands begin to shake. She grabbed the test and stared at it in shock, hardly believing her eyes. F. It was enclosed in a big red circle. She flipped to the second page. The blank answer spaces beside most of the essay questions had left the teacher plenty of room to jot a note in red. *Nice try on #1*, she had written. *But you forgot to mention that the Genteel Tradition began as a movement toward beauty and optimism in literature and the arts. Partial credit. And what happened to the other answers?*

Flipping the test back to the first page, Carole glanced at the grade at the top once more before quickly turning it facedown on her desk. But it was too late. That big, bright F—F, as in *fail, flunk, fool*—was emblazoned in her mind. She felt tears spring into her eyes, and she squeezed them shut to keep the tears from spilling over. It wasn't fair. Why did this have to happen, now of all times? She should have known that things were going too well. She was loving her job, making real progress with Samson, and feeling good about

129

everything at the stable, from helping with the new riders to assisting Max and Judy with Prancer. And now school had to intrude, to ruin everything. It just wasn't fair.

She could hardly concentrate on anything her teacher said for the rest of the class period. For once she wasn't distracted by thoughts of Samson and his training. She was busy trying to figure out a way out of this mess.

One thing she knew for sure: Max wasn't going to make an exception for her. There was no way around that. If Carole's overall grade fell below a C—and this early in the marking period, one test could do it—that was it. Once Ms. Shepard reported that grade to the vice principal, the vice principal would call Pine Hollow. And once Max knew that Carole had slipped below the cutoff, he would ban her from the stable, allowing her only to feed and groom Starlight, if she was lucky. Carole didn't think she could stand that.

She hadn't figured out a solution by the time Ms. Shepard dismissed the class. The only plan she had come up with was to call Stevie as soon as she got home and beg for her help. Stevie had always been good at wriggling her way out of tight situations and finding creative answers to sticky problems. Maybe she could help Carole out of this one, though Carole couldn't begin to imagine how.

"Carole," Ms. Shepard said as Carole started to gather her books. "Don't forget, I want to talk to you."

"I know," Carole replied heavily. She stuffed her books—and the test—into her backpack, then walked slowly toward the teacher's desk. A few of her classmates gave her curious looks on their way out, but Carole avoided their eyes. She just wanted to get this over with, to find out where she really stood.

She stopped in front of Ms. Shepard's desk and waited, eyes downcast, until the rest of the class had gone. Then she looked the teacher in the face. "I'm really sorry, Ms. Shepard," she blurted out, not sure what she was going to say until she heard herself saying it. "I know I messed up on that test. But—But I just need another chance. Maybe if I took a retest—"

"Carole." Ms. Shepard held up a hand to stop her. "Please, I have a few things I want to say first. I just want to make sure you realize that this is a serious matter. Your grades up to this point have been adequate, but hardly stellar. This test is going to make a real dent in your semester average so far."

Carole chewed on her lip again. "How much of a dent?"

The teacher glanced down at the grade book on her desk. "Well, I haven't worked out the numbers yet," she admitted. "But if I had to take a guess, I'd say that once I average in this grade, you'll barely be passing."

Carole's whole body seemed to go cold at the teacher's words. This was worse than she'd thought. If her average was a D– or even a D, it would be difficult, if not impossible, to bring it up before midterms, and those were weeks away. She couldn't let it happen. She just couldn't.

"Ms. Shepard, listen, please," she began, hardly knowing what she was saying. "I know I did really badly on this test, but you have to give me another chance. Please! I'll take a makeup test whenever you say. Just give me one more chance."

Ms. Shepard was already shaking her head. "I'm sorry, Carole," she said. "It just wouldn't be fair to the rest of the—"

"But you don't understand!" Carole cried out. This time, as the tears came, she didn't bother to hold them back. She was too busy trying to come up with an argument that might change the teacher's mind. "I had a lot on my mind this past week, and I just couldn't concentrate. . . ."

Ms. Shepard pulled a box of tissues out of her desk and passed it to Carole, looking concerned. "Oh, dear," the teacher said. "Carole, is there something I should know? Has something been going on lately—something with your family, perhaps?"

Carole blinked. Why did teachers seem to think that students' difficulties always stemmed from family problems? She opened her mouth to try to explain, to convince Ms. Shepard how important this stage of Samson's training was, how delicate Prancer's situation was right now, how much other work there always was to do at the stable.

But before she could form the words, Ms. Shepard had grasped her hand. "You can trust me, Carole." The teacher's words were gentle. "If there are problems at home—some kind of family trouble that kept you from preparing for that test—maybe we can work something out."

Carole hesitated. Was she hearing right? Was the teacher offering her a way out of this mess?

But I can't, she protested silently. *I'm not having any family troubles. Dad hasn't even been at home lately. I can't lie about that.*

Or could she? It would be so easy, and who would really be getting hurt?

Her mouth was forming the words before she realized she'd reached a decision. "Actually, I have been awfully worried about my dad this past week. He's been sick."

"Sick?" Ms. Shepard looked slightly skeptical.

There was no turning back now. Carole took a deep breath and blinked a few times. "I know it doesn't sound like much," she said, her voice quavering a bit from nervousness. She had never knowingly lied to a teacher before, and it made her feel queasy. Still, what choice did she have? "But my mom died a few years ago, and Dad's all I have left . . ."

"Oh, you poor thing." Ms. Shepard rubbed the back of Carole's hand, looking stricken. "I had no idea. I hope he's feeling better now."

Carole nodded. "Oh, he's fine," she said. "Um, I was just pretty tired from, you know . . ." She faltered, wondering how other people did this all the time.

Fortunately, Ms. Shepard had heard enough. "Don't worry about that now, Carole." She dug into the top drawer of her desk, pulling out a calendar. "Let's see when we can schedule a retest, shall we?"

Carole nodded, hardly daring to breathe for fear of ruining things. She couldn't believe this was happening. It was almost too easy.

"Do you have a study hall?" Ms. Shepard asked. "Maybe we could do it then."

"Monday, Wednesday, and Friday fourth period," Carole supplied.

The teacher stared at her calendar. "Hmmm. I have a class then. It might be better to schedule this after school. How about Thursday? That will give you a couple of days to prepare."

Carole shook her head. "I'm sorry. I can't do it

then," she said. Thursdays were one of the days the intermediate riding class met right after school, and this week Max had asked Carole to help him teach the class. "My job . . ."

Ms. Shepard frowned but nodded. "Well, all right," she said. "Then I think it will have to be tomorrow. That won't give you much time to study, but—"

"That's okay," Carole said quickly. She didn't want the teacher to change her mind. Besides, the most important thing was just to get the makeup test over with so that she could stop worrying about it. And there weren't any early-afternoon classes at Pine Hollow on Wednesdays, so it wouldn't matter if she was a little late. She would just have to stay up late reading those chapters tonight, that was all. "Tomorrow would be great. I'll be ready."

That afternoon, as soon as the final bell rang, Lisa made a beeline for her car. She was supposed to be at a yearbook meeting, but she was skipping it. She had something more important to do.

The day before, she had managed to put aside her worries about Prancer long enough to finish her English paper. But afterward, at Callie's party, they had all come rushing back, stronger than ever. That was when she'd realized how ridiculous this situation was. Her fears had been growing steadily for the past few weeks. At first they had been nothing more than a niggling concern, consisting of the kinds of far-out what-if questions her friends were always teasing her about. For that reason, Lisa hadn't allowed herself to pay much attention to them.

But lately those tiny fears had blown up into something much larger until they were consuming her waking thoughts. At this point there was no denying that something serious was happening with Prancer, and Lisa knew that if she didn't find out what it was soon, it really would drive her crazy. She was a little surprised that Max hadn't realized that himself—he knew how much Lisa had always cared for Prancer—but that was neither here nor there. Max had a lot on his mind, a lot of responsibilities: thirty-odd horses, a staff of six or eight people, dozens of students, and a wife and two young daughters. Besides that, Lisa hadn't been spending much time at the stable lately, so it was no wonder if she had slipped his mind.

But now it was time—*past* time—to remind him that she was still around, still needed to know the truth about Prancer. She was determined not to leave the stable that day until she found out everything she wanted to know.

The drive to Pine Hollow didn't take long.

Soon Lisa was pulling into the gravel driveway. As she brought her car to a stop in the parking area, she glanced at the main schooling ring in front of the stable. Red O'Malley, the head stable hand, was trotting around it on Topside, the horse he and Max often rode during lessons.

Good, Lisa thought. *That must mean Red is teaching today's intermediate class, so Max should have plenty of time to talk to me.*

She gave Red a quick wave on her way past. Once inside, she went straight to the stable office, but it was empty. She checked the tack room, which was packed with chattering intermediate students, and the indoor ring, which was empty. Then she began walking around the U-shaped stable row, methodically checking stalls.

She still hadn't found Max by the time she reached Prancer's stall. As she paused to look inside, the sweet bay mare hurried forward, nickering as if pleased to see her.

"Hi there, girl," Lisa said softly, rubbing the mare's velvety dark nose. For a moment she forgot all about confronting Max. It felt so good to see Prancer, even knowing she couldn't ride her, even worrying about what could be wrong with her— just enjoying her unique, familiar, comforting presence.

Lisa couldn't resist opening the door and slip-

ping into the stall with the beautiful Thoroughbred. She didn't have any grooming tools with
her, but suddenly she remembered the small
plastic comb in her jeans pocket. Pulling it out,
she set to work gently untangling Prancer's silky
black mane, simply enjoying the feeling of doing
something useful for the horse she loved.

"How could anything be wrong with you,
Prancer?" she murmured. For the umpteenth
time, she ran her eyes over the mare, from the tips
of her alert ears to the polished dark hooves at the
end of her long, slender legs. She couldn't see
anything that would indicate a health problem.
Prancer stood squarely on all four legs, her coat
was smooth and shiny, her mane and tail were
long and full. There was no sign of discomfort in
her liquid black eyes, and she hadn't lost any
weight as far as Lisa could tell. "It can't be anything terrible if you look this good," Lisa whispered, pausing just long enough to give the horse
a hug around the neck. "You have to be fine."

Prancer nodded wisely as Lisa released her from
the hug, as if agreeing. Still, Lisa didn't feel particularly reassured by her own words. It was all well
and good to tell herself that Prancer must be okay
because she looked okay. But she had learned the
hard way how the world worked. A few years ago,
she would have insisted that her parents' marriage

was healthy because it looked that way. She hadn't seen the breakup coming at all, which had made it all the more difficult to handle when it came. Lisa liked to be prepared. She didn't enjoy surprises the way Stevie and Alex did. That was why she had to know exactly what was going on with Prancer.

Now that she was here in Prancer's stall, though, her sense of urgency had faded slightly. Lisa wasn't a procrastinator by nature. She would find out the truth today; she had decided that. But first she would spend a few final moments in blissful ignorance, putting her fears and theories out of her mind and simply grooming her favorite horse as if nothing in the world had changed.

Lisa wasn't sure how many minutes passed as she picked at Prancer's mane, working more slowly than usual because the weak plastic teeth of her comb weren't made for the relatively coarse hair of a horse. After a while she became vaguely aware that much of the commotion out in the aisles had died down, which meant the intermediate riding lesson had started. But she didn't pay much attention to that. She was focused on Prancer. In all the rush and tumult of the new school year, Lisa had almost forgotten what it meant to simply spend time with the mare like this. To sink into these wordless, timeless periods of just being together, surrounded by the wonderful, comforting sounds and smells of the stable, recalling why she had loved horses and riding so much in the first place. She hadn't even realized how much she had missed it until this very moment. Now all she wanted to do was enjoy it and appreciate it as long as she could . . .

"Lisa." The sudden intrusion of a human voice startled her. She glanced at the stall door and saw Max standing outside.

Suddenly everything came back to her in a rush. This was the moment she'd been waiting for. It was time to find out the truth.

She walked to the door. When she got there, she saw that Max wasn't alone. Clinging to his hand was his four-year-old daughter, Maxi, her wide blue eyes a perfect mirror of his own.

"Oh. Hi there, Maxi." Lisa smiled at the little girl.

"Hi, Lisa!" Maxi chirped brightly. Maxi—short for Maxine—was an outgoing child who loved to talk to anybody. While her quieter, shyer little sister, Jean, invariably known as Minnie, sometimes seemed frightened by the sheer size of the horses, Maxi loved visiting the stable as often as she could. She had always loved riding in the saddle in front of her father, and recently she had started learning to ride in earnest, looking very tiny even perched aboard Krona, Pine Hollow's newest and smallest pony.

Lisa noticed that Max wore a worried expression as he glanced from her to Prancer and back again. She took a deep breath. She would have preferred not to have this confrontation in front of Maxi, but it just couldn't wait any longer.

"Listen, Max," she said, letting herself out of the stall so that she could face him directly. "I'm glad you're here. We need to talk."

Max glanced at his watch, looking uncharacteristically nervous. "Can it wait, Lisa? I have a lot to—"

"This can't wait," Lisa interrupted. "I need to know what's going on with Prancer. You know I care about her, and if anything's seriously wrong . . ."

"I told you before, you shouldn't worry." Max shifted his weight from one foot to the other, looking uncomfortable. He stared off at a spot somewhere just above Lisa's left shoulder. "As you know, my only concern is for the best conditions for the horses in my care, and I have to use my own judgment to provide that. Now, in Prancer's case, I've decided that the best thing for her at this point in time is to remove her from the regular riding rotation for a while, until such a time that I feel—"

Lisa opened her mouth to interrupt again, feeling annoyed at Max's long-winded, roundabout response. But Maxi beat her to it.

"But, Daddy!" the little girl piped up, tugging at Max's arm. "You said everyone could ride Prancer again. Just not till after she has her babies."

EIGHT

Lisa's jaw dropped. "What?"

Max's face had gone white. "Maxi, honey," he said, kneeling down beside his daughter. "Why don't you go down to my office and wait for me there? You can look at that big horse book you like with all the pictures, as long as you promise to turn the pages very carefully. I'll be there in a minute. Okay?"

Maxi nodded agreeably and skipped off down the aisle. Lisa waited until she was gone before she exploded. "You mean all this time you've been acting so mysterious because Prancer is pregnant?"

"Shhh," Max hissed, looking stern. "Keep your voice down, please, Lisa. I don't want the whole stable to hear this." His nervousness had fled and he was his usual self again, brisk and in control. "Now, before you fly off the handle, let me explain."

Lisa crossed her arms over her chest and waited. Her head was spinning and she wasn't sure what to feel: Relief that Prancer wasn't sick? Rage at being kept in the dark so long, so unnecessarily? Curiosity about what Max had to say? Joy that Prancer would be having a foal?

Max didn't keep her in suspense long. "The reason we haven't told anyone about this pregnancy so far is because it's a little unusual," he said. "You see, it seems that Prancer is carrying twins."

That stunned Lisa almost as much as the original news had. "Twins?" she repeated. "But I always thought—"

Max was already nodding. "Twins are very rare in horses—probably only a percentage or two of all pregnancies. And such pregnancies very rarely result in two live foals. Often, as you know, one of the fetuses is naturally aborted. Otherwise, if you catch it early, it's usually possible to remove one of the fetuses manually. But that's really only a practical option for the first two or three weeks, and we didn't find out she was carrying twins until a good four weeks in. That's why we've been waiting and watching, doing what we can to give one or both foals a chance—or at least keep Prancer herself safe."

Lisa already knew most of what Max was telling her. She had studied equine reproduction in Pony Club, and she had observed plenty of pregnancies and births firsthand. But she was still having trouble taking it all in. Because this time, the information wasn't merely academic. It had to do with the health and well-being of Prancer—*her* Prancer.

She tried to will her mind to work, to process it all and figure out what else she needed to know. "You said you found out about the twins four weeks in," she said. "How far along is she now? What does Judy say about her condition? Who else knows about this? What special care will Prancer need from now on? Is there any danger to her own health at this point, or just to the foals? How risky do things look right now?"

Max held up a hand as if to fend off her torrent of questions, smiling slightly. "We bred her—to Geronimo, by the way—in late July," he said. "So that puts us at . . . let's see . . . somewhere around ten weeks. Only Red, Judy Barker, and I knew about the breeding when it happened, and we've only told a couple of other people so far since then, strictly on a need-to-know basis. Until we found out about the twins, I let people keep riding her—you rode her a couple of times after you got back, didn't you? But once we knew, I decided not to let anyone ride her."

Lisa nodded numbly. Late July. That explained why she hadn't had a clue. She had been in California then. If only she had been around, if only she had guessed, she could have saved herself so much needless worry, so much heartache. . . .

She wasn't sure whether to be angry at Max for keeping this from her, or at herself for not making him tell her sooner.

Sensing her distress, Max put a hand on her shoulder. "I'm sorry you were worried, Lisa," he said gently. "I'm sure you can see that I had my reasons for keeping quiet about this, but, well . . . Actually, I'd started thinking lately that it was time you knew. I just wasn't sure how to tell you, and I've been so busy that I haven't had a chance to sit down with Carole and see how she thought we should——"

"Carole?" That broke through Lisa's numbness. She blinked, trying to make sense of what Max had just said. "You mean Carole was one of the people you told? She knew about this?"

Max cleared his throat. "She works here, Lisa," he reminded her gently. "Of course she needed to know."

Carole had known the truth.

That one fact expanded to fill Lisa's mind, pushing aside even her remaining unanswered questions about Prancer. It was just too unbelievable. Her logical mind struggled to reject it. "Carole knew about this, and she just sat back and let me worry?" Lisa's voice rose in pitch again, in concert with her rising anger. Now she knew she had been right not to direct that anger—born of fear, of worry, of countless sleepless hours over the past days and weeks—toward Max or even toward herself. Now she saw who was really to blame. The one person who had known the truth all along and had also known how worried she was. The person Lisa had trusted, the person who could have reassured her weeks ago but had decided not to do so. The best friend who had let Lisa stew, had listened to her worry and wonder, had watched her agonize over this—and said nothing. Carole. It couldn't be true, but somehow, horribly, it was.

All these thoughts flung themselves through Lisa's mind in seconds. When she spoke again, her voice was quieter but still filled with anguish. "I can't believe she would do this to me!"

She clenched her fists at her sides, her whole body feeling cold and foreign to her. Lisa didn't lose her temper very often, but on the rare occasions when her emotions spun out of control, she often felt as though she were standing at the center of a hurricane—in a cool, still, eerily calm eye surrounded by a deadly, howling storm just waiting to consume her.

Max looked worried. "Lisa, it's not Carole's fault," he began. "I asked her not to tell anyone. I made her promise . . ."

But Lisa didn't hear the rest of what he had to say. The storm was taking over, making her blind

147

and deaf to everything else. She had already whirled around and was racing down the aisle.

Carole ran a rub rag briskly over Starlight's coat. "Almost done, boy," she murmured, giving the horse an absentminded pat on the neck. She had just brought him in from the back paddock. She'd called Red between classes to ask him to turn him out there for a while. That way she wouldn't have to spend any time exercising him that day. Even so, she knew she would have to hurry if she wanted to get everything done and still get home in time to put in a solid night of studying for her makeup history test. *That test* . . . Carole still couldn't believe she had messed up so badly. She also couldn't believe she had to waste more hours studying American history. As if school didn't already take up too much of her time . . .

Luckily, Red was taking care of the intermediate riders, who would be finishing their lesson before long, and Ben had volunteered to take Firefly, a young mare he and Carole were training, out on the trail in lieu of a more structured session. That meant all Carole had to do was give Starlight a quick grooming, look in on Prancer, and take care of the rest of her regular stable chores before moving on to her final and most anticipated task— Samson.

Her mind had already wandered ahead to the black horse's workout. Today she planned to work on the flat, concentrating on Samson's suppleness. He seemed to get bigger and more muscular with each day they worked together, and she wanted to make sure that his steadily increasing strength wouldn't compromise his ability to move well in all directions, to take the sharp turns that were sometimes required in show jumping. Therefore, she had planned out a course of fairly challenging serpentines that the two of them could perform in the indoor ring.

I'm sure Samson won't have any trouble with the serpentines, though, Carole thought as she mechanically continued Starlight's grooming. *He did brilliantly when I worked with him on the same thing after he first arrived at Pine Hollow. Maybe I ought to throw in a little extra practice on his half-halts, just to keep things interesting, or maybe—*

"Carole!" a harsh, angry voice interrupted her thoughts.

Startled, she glanced up and saw Lisa standing outside the stall. "Oh, hi," Carole greeted her, already scanning her mind. She hadn't promised to go on a trail ride with her friends today, had she? She hoped not—she had enough to do as it was. And she wasn't in the mood for more of their teasing about her forgetfulness. Not after what had happened in history class. "What's up?"

"We need to talk," Lisa said coldly. "Right now!"

Carole frowned, put off by her imperious tone. *Just what I need after the day I had at school,* she thought petulantly. *Straight-A Lisa stopping by to start bossing me around.* "Can it wait?" she asked bluntly. "I'm kind of busy here."

"Too bad." Lisa's voice was edged with steel. "You and I have a big problem right now. Or rather, *I* have a big problem, and it's you."

Carole was starting to get really annoyed—she hated it when Lisa began talking like a stern, disapproving teacher—but then Lisa's words sank in. Confused, Carole turned to face her. For the first time she noticed the enraged expression on Lisa's face. "Um, what?" she said uncertainly, caught between irritation and concern. "What are you talking about? I—"

"I just talked to Max." Lisa's words came in such a furious rush that they were a little difficult for Carole to follow. "He told me everything, including the fact that you've known what's going on for ages now and you never told me a thing. You didn't even let me know that you knew. I had to figure it out for myself, after I'd made myself half sick worrying about Prancer—"

"Prancer?" Carole interrupted with a sinking feeling. Now she realized what this was about. Max had finally told Lisa about Prancer's pregnancy. But why did she look so angry? Carole had guessed she would be kind of annoyed when she found out that Carole and Max had been keeping secrets, but Lisa was a rational person—almost too rational sometimes. She had to understand why they had done it. Didn't she? "Listen, Lisa. I wanted to tell you, but I—"

"No, you listen to me." Lisa's voice shook. "I trusted you, Carole. When I asked you if you knew what was going on, you lied to me. You stood there and *lied*, right to my face!"

Carole took an abrupt step back from the stall door, stung by Lisa's tirade. What was her problem? Behind her, Starlight tossed his head and shifted his feet, obviously a bit nervous about all the yelling.

"I didn't lie, not exactly," Carole returned quickly. "I mean, I didn't mean to. If you'll just let me explain, I can—"

"I don't want to hear it," Lisa said, her voice as venomous as Carole had ever heard it. "You've had weeks to explain, weeks while I was going crazy with worry, and you blew it, Carole. You totally blew it."

Carole didn't know what to say. She couldn't believe the way Lisa was acting. It was scary to see her so angry, so clearly out of control, especially since Liza was usually the calmest and most logical person she knew. Didn't Lisa understand that

151

Carole had a job here, a responsibility to her boss? Besides, how was she supposed to know that Lisa was so all-fired worried? It certainly didn't show. Lisa had hardly bothered to stop by the stable for weeks as far as Carole could recall. "You don't know what you're talking about."

"I know enough," Lisa shot back. "I know you just proved you really do care more about horses than people. You betrayed me, and real friends don't do that."

Carole clenched her fists. There was that tone again: uptight, judgmental, certain. Lisa was always so sure that she was right and everyone who didn't think exactly the way she did was wrong. That might work for her in school, but it could be infuriating in real life. Just because she had spent her life being told how perfect she was—by teachers, by other adults, by just about *everyone*—that didn't mean she knew what was best in every situation. After all their years of friendship, wasn't she even going to give Carole a chance to tell her side of the story? "Oh yeah? Well, real friends don't get hysterical and start insulting people for no reason, either!" Carole cried. "Especially when those people were just trying to do the right thing. So what kind of friend are you?"

"Aaah!" Lisa shut her eyes tightly for a moment then opened them and glared at Carole. "I can't believe you're trying to turn this back on me. Do you ever listen to yourself?"

At that, Carole felt hot, angry tears welling up in her eyes. This couldn't be happening, could it? It had to be some kind of crazy nightmare. Was she really having this awful, ugly fight with one of her best friends? She willed herself not to let her tears spill over. The last thing she wanted to do was start crying in front of Lisa right now. "If I'm such a horrible person, then why are you hanging around here?" she asked as coldly as she could manage. "Maybe you should just leave, since you've obviously already made up your mind about this. I'm not exactly enjoying this lecture, and I've got work to do."

Lisa's eyes narrowed for a moment; then she took a step backward. "Fine." She spun on her heel and stormed away. After a few steps, she paused just long enough to fling one final remark over her shoulder. "It's a good thing you're such great pals with all the horses here. At this rate, they'll be the only friends you have left."

Callie rolled over on her bed and glanced at her closed bedroom door. "Listen, I should probably go soon," she whispered into the phone. "I've been up here for a while, and if I don't watch out, Mom will start in on me with her we-have-a-guest speech."

"Okay," Stevie replied from the other end of the line. "But don't give up on this, okay? You just have to make that first breakthrough happen, and I bet after that the rest will take care of itself. It'll be easy. And all you have to do to get things rolling is put yourself out there, be honest with her. I know you can do it."

"Thanks, Stevie." Callie swung her legs over the edge of the bed and glanced down at her crutches, which were leaning against her old oak bureau. "I certainly hope you're right."

"Remember," Stevie added, "you're the only one who can make this happen. If you want it, you've got to go for it."

Callie couldn't help smiling at that. It sounded exactly like something her old endurance coach back home in Valley Vista might have said before a race. "You're right about that," she said. "I'll let you know how it goes."

"You'd better," Stevie warned.

Callie said good-bye and leaned over to replace the black cordless phone on its base on the bureau. Then she grabbed her crutches and headed for the door.

She found Sheila in the large, level, fenced-in backyard, sitting in a lounge chair watching Scott, who was playing with the family dog on the wide swath of grass beyond the pool.

Callie lowered herself onto the chair beside her

and took a deep breath. "Hi, Sheila," she said, already feeling uncomfortable. "How's it going?"

Sheila turned to glance at her, removing the dark sunglasses she was wearing. "I don't know what you were complaining about in all those letters," she said, stretching lazily on the lounge chair. "The weather here isn't bad at all. It's actually kind of nice."

"Of course it's beautiful now. It's October already, remember? I wrote you those letters in July and August," Callie replied. "Back then the humidity was about ninety-nine percent, and the temperature hit triple digits a couple of times." She grimaced, remembering how uncomfortable all that oppressive, prickly heat had felt, especially when her leg was trapped in a thick fabric brace for part of the time. "Believe me, that's when I was really missing that mountain climate back home."

There was a shout and a flurry of barks from across the lawn as Scott playfully tackled the dog. "What kind of dog is Wendell again?" Sheila asked, shielding her eyes against the afternoon sunlight as the furry brown-and-white dog leaped after the tennis ball Scott had just lobbed across the yard. "I can never remember."

So far this conversation wasn't going quite the way Callie had intended it to. Here they were, wasting their one full afternoon together trading small talk. Callie didn't want to let it go on any longer. It was now or never. "She's an Australian shepherd," she said. "But listen, Sheila. I just wanted to say I'm really glad—um, you know, that you could stop by and visit."

Sheila glanced at her and shrugged. "Hey, me too," she replied, slipping her sunglasses back on and crossing one leg over the other. "If I had to stay in one more bad hotel room on this trip, I probably would have screamed. Chez Forester is *très* more chic."

That wasn't exactly the response Callie had been hoping for. *"You're the only one who can make this happen."* Stevie's words floated through her mind.

"That's not really what I meant," Callie said. "I just meant that it's really great to see you, Sheila. I've missed you. It's weird not hanging out with you all the time, you know?"

Sheila glanced at her. Even behind her sunglasses, her face registered surprise. "Hey, that's sweet, Callie," she replied, sounding uncertain. "I've missed you, too."

That gave Callie strength to plunge forward. "Actually, I've missed you a lot. It's been even harder than I expected, moving to a brand-new place where I don't know anyone except my family."

"Well, sure." Sheila shrugged. "I mean, the accident and everything—"

"It wasn't just that," Callie interrupted. "I mean, in a way that almost made it easier. Does that sound weird?" Sheila merely shrugged again, so Callie continued. "I mean, I wouldn't have chosen to do it that way, but it kind of helped break the ice. Made people look at me as something other than the congressman's daughter, you know?"

Sheila peered at her over the tops of her sunglasses. "I thought you liked being the congressman's daughter."

Callie shook her head slowly. She and Sheila had a lot of ground to make up. "I'm not surprised you thought that," she said. "It's what I always wanted everyone to think, because I knew there wasn't anything I could do about it anyway." She took a deep breath. "But actually, I hate it. I hate feeling different, having people watch everything I do and say because of Dad's job. Sometimes it makes me want to scream, or dye my hair purple, or just do something really crazy."

"I had no idea," Sheila murmured, looking thoughtful. She sat up in her chair and gazed at Callie. "You should have told me this sooner. I mean, we're friends, right?"

Callie felt her heart lift at that. Stevie had been

right. This was probably the deepest, most meaningful conversation she and Sheila had ever had. And even though starting it had been difficult, it really was getting easier with every word. It still felt strange, almost unreal and a little scary to be talking to Sheila about her true thoughts and feelings. But it also gave her an exhilarating feeling of freedom and power. For the first time she could speak out, bare her soul to someone who had known her forever, without worrying about trying to sound cool or keeping the upper hand. Why had she been so uptight, so snobby and overcautious? Why hadn't she trusted Sheila before this?

"I wish I had told you sooner," she told Sheila. "I really do. You might be the only one who's known us long enough to see that it's not always easy being a member of my family." She waved a hand at Scott, who was playing tug-of-war with Wendell over near the rosebushes. "I mean, take my brother, for example. Everyone thinks he's so perfect and cheerful all the time, but I know better. And Mom—"

"What do you mean?" Sheila interrupted. "Don't tell me good old Cookie is as angst-ridden as the rest of us ordinary teens."

Callie smiled. Sheila had always had a unique way of putting things. "He's not that bad, mostly," she admitted. "I just get kind of fed up sometimes with his Mr. Perfect persona, you know? I mean, one time . . ." She trailed off and glanced over at Scott, who was well out of earshot. "I probably shouldn't tell you this."

"Tell me what?" Sheila demanded. "Come on, you know you can trust me."

Callie pursed her lips uncertainly, but she couldn't resist Sheila's earnest expression. *This is what trust is about, right?* she thought, taking a deep breath. "Well, okay," she relented. "But you can't let anyone—especially Scott—know that I told." At Sheila's nod, she went on. "One time last year, Scott's debate team lost this big competition by, like, two points or something." She shrugged. "Actually, I don't know how they score those things. But it was close."

"I think I remember that." Sheila nodded thoughtfully. "Cookie looked a little depressed for about a day, then he snapped out of it."

"But that wasn't really all." Callie checked once more to make sure there was no way Scott could hear. He didn't even know she knew about this, and she wanted to keep it that way. "The night of the debate, Mom and Dad were out at some function or other. I'd just finished a really tough workout at the stable, and I was zonked on the couch. I guess Scott thought I was asleep, or maybe he didn't see me at all. But I saw him sneak into the dining room and take a bottle of Scotch out of the liquor cabinet."

Sheila's eyebrows shot up above the rims of her sunglasses. "No way!" she breathed.

Callie had kept this incident bottled up inside herself for so long that it was a relief to tell someone else about it. "He disappeared up to his room and I didn't see him again, and the next day that bottle was back where it belonged. Half empty."

"Didn't your folks notice?"

"No way." Callie shrugged. "Don't you remember? They're always having those impromptu cocktail parties whenever someone important drops by. And most of their friends drink like fish. There's no way they could ever keep track of every bottle."

Sheila shook her head slowly. "Amazing," she said. "Was that the only time you saw him do something like that?"

"Yeah." Callie sighed. "I just hope it was only that one time, you know?" She bit her lip, feeling the minor but nagging worry rise again. "I mean, Scott doesn't usually even drink at parties or anything. So it was probably just a one-time thing, right? Sort of an experiment."

"I'm sure it was." Sheila's eyes were sympathetic. "Anyway, I'm starting to see what you mean about your family. I've known you guys forever, but I guess you never really know anyone until you live with them, huh?"

Callie rolled her eyes. "Tell me about it," she

said. "If Dad's constituents could hear the way he jokes around about them—or better yet, if the other congressmen on his new welfare committee could hear the way he makes fun of them at the dinner table . . ." She giggled. "There's one guy he always calls Congressman Buffoon, and another he likes to compare to moss . . ."

Sheila laughed. "That's hysterical," she declared. "Which congressmen are they? Anyone I've heard of?"

Callie grimaced. "I don't know, I can't keep track. Anyway, Dad just joined this committee recently. He was all excited about it because he thinks welfare is such a hot topic right now. He's sure it will help his career a lot."

"It probably will," Sheila agreed. "I guess moving the whole family out here to the East Coast probably didn't hurt him either, did it?"

"I guess," Callie said. "He really seems to love it here. Sometimes I think he doesn't miss Valley Vista at all." She sighed. "I sure do, though. Every day. I miss the mountains, and the coastline. I miss Coach Clemson and the rest of the people at the old stable, and I miss those rocky trails where I used to train. I miss shopping at the Vista Mall, where I knew all the stores, and hanging out in the school parking lot, sitting on the hood of Richard Fisher's car with you and Jessica and Mel and the rest of the gang."

"Just don't try to tell me you miss Mr. Trainor's geometry class," Sheila warned. "Otherwise I'll know you've lost it."

Callie grinned. "Well, I wouldn't go that far," she admitted. She leaned forward, suddenly feeling mischievous and a little bit wicked. "I'll tell you what else I do miss, though," she whispered. "Your cousin Mike. I've had a crush on him for years."

"No way!" Sheila laughed. "Mike? For real? But he's not your type at all."

Callie smiled as she pictured Sheila's cousin. Mike was in his mid-twenties, dark-haired and muscular. He was known as the black sheep of Sheila's family, partly because he had gone to trade school instead of college and now worked as a welder, but mostly because he was famous for brawling in the local bars. "You're right," she said. "He's not my type at all. But there's just something about those biceps of his . . . and the way he wears those faded old jeans . . ."

Sheila shook her head. "I can't believe this," she crowed. "Cool-as-a-cucumber Callie actually has the hots for my loser cousin. This is major news."

"If we still played that newspaper-reporter game we played when we were kids, it could be our lead story," Callie joked. "Remember how we used to plan how we'd be famous journalists someday like Woodward and Bernstein?"

"Sure," Sheila said. "But never mind that. I'm more interested in hearing more about this thing with Mike."

Callie grinned. This felt good. Her relief at not having to censor herself, not having to hold back, was almost overwhelming. There were so many things she wanted to share with Sheila now—important things, confusing things, even silly things like her crush on Mike. *If only Sheila didn't have to leave tomorrow . . .*

NINE

"That's great!" Stevie exclaimed into the phone. "I'm so happy for you, Callie. Okay, I'll see you tomorrow. Bye!"

She hung up the phone, feeling proud of Callie and almost as proud of herself. Callie had just filled her in on her conversation with Sheila. It sounded as though they had made a real breakthrough in their relationship, and Stevie was glad about that. Callie deserved as many true friends as she could get.

"Who was that?" Phil asked, looking up as she walked back into the den.

"You were gone long enough," Alex added, looking disgruntled. He was leaning against the built-in bookshelves, tossing an apple from hand to hand.

"Sorry about that. It was Callie. She had to tell me something." Stevie flopped down on the sofa beside Phil. "So did you guys have any brilliant brainstorms while I was gone?"

Phil shook his head ruefully. "Not even close," he admitted. "We were just talking about how long A.J.'s weird behavior has been going on."

"It's been longer than I realized," Alex put in, rubbing his apple against his shirt. "With school starting and everything, I didn't even realize it, but he broke up with Julianna like four weeks ago."

Stevie let out a low whistle. "That is a long time," she agreed solemnly. "Way too long. So what are we going to do about it?"

"What can we do?" Phil sighed. "He made it pretty clear yesterday that he isn't interested in talking."

Stevie didn't like the helpless, almost resigned tone of Phil's voice. She hated seeing him so worried about his friend and not being able to do anything to help. "If he won't tell us what's wrong, we'll just have to figure it out another way," she said with determination. "I mean, there are only so many things that could be bothering him, right? So let's come up with a few theories."

"If we were talking about anyone but A.J. here," Alex said slowly, "the first thing I'd think is that maybe he's gotten himself mixed up in drugs or drinking or something like that. But he isn't that kind of guy."

"No way," Phil said quickly. "He's never even taken a swig of beer at a party, as far as I know."

Then he paused. "Still," he said, "I guess we have to put it on our list, right? I mean, just to be thorough or whatever. Right?"

Stevie didn't answer. She didn't even like to think about the possibility that A.J. could be involved in anything like that. "What else?" she asked. "How about some kind of health problem? Maybe he just found out he has cancer or something horrible like that."

Alex nodded thoughtfully. "Could be, though I hope not. It wouldn't necessarily have to be anything as bad as cancer, though. Maybe it's something minor, like he's never going to get any taller, or he's allergic to girls or whatever." He grinned. "Not that that last one would be minor."

Stevie rolled her eyes. "I guess it's possible it could be something medical," she said dubiously. Even though she had brought it up in the first place, the more she thought about it, the more it seemed like a long shot. Still, she supposed they had to consider every possibility. "What else?" She turned to Phil. "Has he been having any trouble at school lately?"

"You mean his grades?" Phil shrugged. "As far as I know they're the same as always."

"I was thinking more of the other kids," Stevie said. "You know—bullies or whatever."

"Oh." Phil thought about that for a second. "I haven't noticed anything. But A.J. used to have

166

some trouble with that because he's always been short and skinny. Maybe it *has* started up again."

Alex was looking skeptical. "Bullies? Grades?" he said. "Come on. Do you really think any of that would totally change his personality? You might as well suggest that he just developed embarrassing body odor. I mean, unless you guys are exaggerating—"

"We're not," Stevie interrupted firmly. "A.J. is totally weird. But you're right. It would take something huge to do that to him."

She paused, trying once again to imagine what could make a person like A.J. change so dramatically. Was there anything that could make *her* change that much? She didn't think so. As long as she had her family, her friends, her health—and as far as they knew, A.J. still had all those things— what could really be so horrible?

"I hate to say it," she said reluctantly, "but I can't think of anything more likely than what you guys said before. You know. Drugs." She had to force the word out, and it tasted sour on her tongue. "If we're going to rule out alien abductions, there's really not much else it could be, is there?"

"I'm surprised you didn't suggest he's just having trouble with his horse," Alex teased, but his heart clearly wasn't in it. He sighed. "I can't be-

167

lieve A.J. could be into something so stupid. It's not like him."

"Nothing about him is like him anymore," Phil reminded Alex, his face more white and strained than ever. "I think we have to be realistic here. We shouldn't jump to any conclusions, but I think we've all seen this movie of the week before, right?"

Alex nodded. "So what do we do now?"

Stevie was already thinking about that. "I think we have to try to talk to him again," she said slowly. "Someone has to try to get through to him, especially if he is mixed up with drugs. And the sooner the better. Do you think we should try going over there again?"

Phil shook his head. "I have a better idea," he said. "Let's try to get him out of his room and into the real world. Maybe then we'll have a better shot at making him listen." He stood up. "I'll call him, see if I can convince him to come hang out at my place with the three of us tomorrow."

"Good idea," Alex agreed. He grinned weakly, clearly not looking forward to the confrontation. "Maybe we can get a bunch of his friends together, you know, sort of like a surprise party."

"Or an intervention!" Stevie blurted out. She sat up straight, surprised that she hadn't thought of it sooner. "You know—like you see on TV sometimes. We gather everyone A.J. knows in one room, then when he gets there and sees a whole crowd instead of just a couple of people, and he finds out how worried we all are, he spills his guts."

Phil looked interested. "That's not a bad idea," he said. "He couldn't possibly ignore all of us, right? I'll go call him right now." He hurried through the arched doorway into the kitchen, and a moment later he was speaking urgently into the phone.

Stevie leaned back against the sofa cushions, not even bothering to strain her ears to hear what Phil was saying. She was sure he would manage to talk A.J. into coming over to his house somehow. Besides, she was busy feeling pleased with her own brilliant plan. As soon as she'd thought of it, she had been positive it would work. *I'm really on a roll this week,* she thought giddily. *First I help Callie bond with her oldest pal, and now this . . .*

Phil was back a few minutes later. "That was easier than I thought," he said, looking more optimistic than Stevie had seen him in weeks. "He's coming over tomorrow after school. Well, actually it will be after he gets out of detention." He shook his head grimly. "It seems he skipped a few classes last week that I didn't know about. Anyway, I didn't even mention that you two would be there, just said something about shooting some hoops."

169

"Good." Stevie rubbed her hands together eagerly. "Once he's there, we won't let him leave until we know the score. Now all we have to do is make sure everyone else shows up. Let's start calling people."

"I'll call Lisa," Alex volunteered quickly.

Stevie smirked. "I don't know," she teased. "We have a lot of other people to call, and we can't have you tying up the phone with all your lovey-dovey smoochy-poochy talk all afternoon."

"Very funny," Alex said sourly. "I'll be right back." He headed for the door, but instead of stopping by the wall phone in the kitchen, he continued straight on through to the front hallway.

"Where's he going?" Phil asked in surprise.

Stevie grinned. "He doesn't want us to listen to him sweet-talking Lisa," she said. "He's probably heading for the extension in the living room. Just for that, we should go listen in on the kitchen phone."

"I have a better idea." Phil turned and wrapped his arms around her. "Since we seem to have a few minutes alone . . ."

Stevie giggled and fluttered her eyelashes at him. "Whatever could you be thinking of, handsome sir?"

Just then Phil's gaze shifted back to the entrance to the room. "Oops," he said, pulling away quickly. "We have company. Hi, Michael."

Michael hovered in the doorway, looking slightly embarrassed. "Uh, hey," he replied with a quick nod at Phil. "Um, I was just wondering if you guys were planning to, you know, go anywhere."

Stevie glared at her younger brother, annoyed at his untimely interruption. "What are you talking about?"

Michael shrugged. "You know, today. Aren't you guys going out to that stupid stable or the ice cream place or anything?"

"Sorry, buddy," Phil said with a wink at Stevie. "We're not going anywhere anytime soon. So I guess your wild party will have to wait, unless we're invited."

Michael rolled his eyes. "Ha, ha," he said sarcastically. He tugged at the lock of hair that hung down over his eyes. "I was just wondering if you were going anywhere, that's all. No biggie."

"Well, you can stop wondering," Stevie told him. "Like Phil said, you're stuck with us. We've got stuff to do here. Anyway, Mom and Dad specifically asked Alex and me to stay here and babysit our baby brother until they get home from work." She grinned, knowing that would bother him, even though he knew as well as she did that it wasn't true.

"You're *soooo* funny, Stevie." Michael scowled and rolled his eyes again. Then he turned and hurried out of the room.

Phil gazed after him, looking curious. "He really seemed anxious for us to leave," he commented. "Wonder what that's all about?"

Stevie snuggled against him. "Who cares?" she said. "But now that he's gone, where were we again?"

Phil grinned. "Right about here," he said, pulling her closer and bending to kiss her.

Their lips had barely touched when Alex raced into the room, panting. "Yo, break it up," he said briskly. "Stevie, I just got off the phone with Lisa."

Stevie glanced at her brother and saw that his face was flushed and he looked distressed. Her heart jumped. "What is it?" she asked immediately. "What's wrong?"

"Lisa's *really* upset," Alex reported, sinking into the big easy chair near the couch. "She just got home from the stable. It sounds like she and Carole had some really huge fight. Lisa claims she's never going to speak to her again, says Carole lied to her face and betrayed her, called her uptight and a bunch of other stuff, and there was something about Prancer in there, too—"

"What?" Stevie was already on her feet. "I can't believe it. Are you sure?"

Alex shrugged. "Hey, I'm not saying she was totally coherent," he said. "But something's going on, and since it has to do with Carole . . ."

"Thanks." Stevie immediately understood what he was saying, and she appreciated it. She knew her brother was very protective of Lisa, but this time he'd realized that Stevie should be the one to try to help her. "I'll go call her right now."

She raced into the kitchen and grabbed the phone off the hook. But a voice squawked at her from the other end. "Hang up!" Michael said peevishly. "I'm on the phone."

"Where are you?" Stevie snapped. "I need to make a call."

"I'm in Mom and Dad's room, and I don't care." Michael sounded defensive even through the phone wires. "You know the rule. You can't make me hang up unless I've been talking more than twenty minutes, and I just got on like two seconds ago."

Want to bet I can't make you hang up, you little squirt? Stevie thought grimly. But she didn't bother to repeat the threat out loud. She didn't have time to fight with her brother right then— she had to find out what had happened between her two best friends. She slammed the phone down and headed for the back door. Lisa lived only half a block away, and from the sound of things this might be a story she needed to hear face-to-face. "I'm going over there," she shouted to Alex and Phil on her way out. "I'll be back when I can."

TEN

A few minutes later Stevie was sitting on the edge of the four-poster bed in Lisa's room. The room hadn't changed much in the years Stevie had known Lisa. It was still tastefully decorated in white and pale, subtle shades of rose, with large windows and wide wooden floorboards. Everything from the desk to the bookcases to the bedspread looked neat and tailored and tidy, just as Lisa herself usually was. At the moment, however, Lisa wasn't looking quite as together as she usually did. Her eyes were red-rimmed from crying, and her hair looked windblown and tangled.

Stevie was frowning. Lisa had just given her a quick description of her fight with Carole, and Stevie was having trouble understanding what the big deal was. "Okay, let me get this straight," she said. "You're never going to speak to her again because . . . why, exactly? What am I missing?"

Lisa blew out a breath, looking frustrated. "Don't you get it?" she asked. "She lied to me.

She kept Prancer's pregnancy a secret and pretended not to know anything, even when I asked her about it."

Stevie was still pretty surprised about Prancer's twin pregnancy, but she pushed that thought aside for the moment. First she had to straighten out this thing between Lisa and Carole. She took a deep breath. "Okay, I can see how that's kind of . . . well, kind of annoying or whatever. But look, she didn't tell me anything, either. So it's not like she was keeping a secret just from you. Max probably asked her not to tell anybody. And you know Carole hates breaking promises and stuff like that."

"That's not the point." Lisa's eyes were watery. She blinked and let out a loud sniffle. "Even if Max did that, Carole should have talked him into telling me. She knew how upset and worried I was. I mean, I really thought Prancer must be d-d-dying or something. And she just let me s-suffer. Would a real friend do that? Would she just stand by and not even *try* to help?"

That made Stevie stop and think. She remembered how worried Lisa had been the other day when she'd confided her fears about Prancer's health. Suddenly she started to understand why Lisa was so upset. It wasn't just the fact that Carole had kept something from her. It was that her secret had actually been harmful, had caused Lisa serious anguish and fear—anguish and fear that a few simple words could have prevented. That wasn't like Carole at all, which made it even stranger, more horrible. Carole must have realized that Lisa would wonder and worry about Prancer's mysterious near-quarantine—Lisa was a worrier by nature, and Carole knew that. She should have seen that Lisa would manage to come up with every awful, fatal ailment in the world and imagine that Prancer had them all.

"You're right. I can't believe she did that," Stevie murmured thoughtfully, shaking her head. "She knows you're not blind. You obviously knew something was up with Prancer—"

"Of course she did," Lisa snapped, rubbing at her eyes with her fist. "I told you. I talked to her about it—more than once. Including just yesterday at school."

"Really?" Stevie frowned, trying to make sense of what she was hearing, to fit it into some pattern of behavior she could understand. What was going on with Carole? How could she have treated one of her best friends this way?

Thinking about it just didn't seem like enough all of a sudden. It was time to take action. Stevie hopped off the bed and headed for the door.

"Where are you going?" Lisa asked.

Stevie paused and turned, her face grim. "I'm going to have a little talk with our friend Carole," she said. "I want to see what she has to say for herself."

Carole hooked Starlight's water bucket to its metal ring on the back wall of the stall. "There you go, boy," she told her horse as he curiously stuck his nose into the bucket, snuffling at the water and making a light spray fly out and splash Carole's arm.

She smiled automatically at the gelding's antics. But her mind wasn't really on Starlight. Earlier, after that unpleasant encounter with Lisa, Carole had been so disconcerted that she had no longer been able to concentrate on her grooming job. Instead, she had left Starlight half groomed and moved on to something she knew would distract her—Samson's training.

That had done the trick. The big black horse always seemed to be able to take her mind off her problems, and today, by the end of their strenuous sixty-minute workout, Carole had felt almost giddy.

That had ended when she'd put Samson away and returned to Starlight's stall. She had finished his interrupted grooming and was now making him comfortable for the evening. But all the while, her mind had been busily turning over what Lisa had said to her earlier, the horrible

178

things she had accused her of. The worst part was, she hadn't even let Carole try to explain . . .

As Carole brushed the droplets off her arm and turned away from the water bucket, she was so lost in thought that she hardly heard the rapid footsteps approaching in the aisle outside. But she could hardly miss Stevie's red, sweaty face as it appeared over the top of the stall's wooden half door.

"What's the big idea?" Stevie demanded without preamble.

Carole glanced at her in surprise. "Are you okay?" she asked. "You seem a little out of breath."

Stevie brushed aside the comment without bothering to respond. She had run all the way to Pine Hollow from Lisa's house, turning a fifteen-minute walk into a five-minute sprint. But that was the last thing she felt like discussing at the moment. "I just came from Lisa's place. She's really upset."

"She's not the only one," Carole muttered with a grimace.

Stevie hesitated, surprised. She had expected Carole to be either clueless or contrite about what had happened. "What do you mean?" she asked cautiously.

Starlight had turned to snuffle at Carole's shoulder, and she reached up to put an arm around the gelding's neck, seeming to take strength from the horse while playing absently with his mane. "I suppose she told you what happened."

"She said you knew about Prancer's pregnancy for ages and you didn't tell her. She said she was worried sick, but when she tried to talk to you about it, you brushed her off and let her keep worrying."

Carole frowned, her cheeks deepening to an angry red. "Well, there's some stuff she *didn't* tell you," she said. "I know that, because she didn't stick around long enough to listen to my side of the story. Should I even bother to tell you, or have you already made up your mind, too?"

"Oh." Stevie felt a twinge of shame, realizing that Carole's accusation was hitting pretty close to home. Stevie had made up her mind, and that wasn't fair. There were two sides to every story, and as clear-cut as Lisa's grievance seemed to her, Carole deserved to be heard, too. After so many years of living in a house with two lawyers as parents, Stevie should have known better. "Okay. Sorry," she said penitently. "What happened?"

Her words seemed to calm Carole down immediately. She gave Starlight one final pat, then stepped forward and let herself out of the stall so that she was facing Stevie in the stable aisle. "I did know about Prancer's condition. Max told me a

few weeks ago," she began evenly. "From the beginning, I had trouble keeping it to myself. I
really wanted to tell you guys—especially Lisa, for
obvious reasons." She took a deep breath. "But
Max is my boss. And you know I take my job here
seriously. He really didn't want anyone else to
know that early, since it was Prancer's first pregnancy and there's no telling what can happen with
twins. If word got out, there's no way we could
keep her from getting mobbed by concerned Pony
Clubbers, and Judy thought it was important to
keep her calm, and—well, you get the picture. I
could sort of tell that Lisa was wondering, and
that made me feel really bad, but I—"

Carole paused as George Wheeler, a rider their
age, turned the corner of the aisle and walked
toward them. She snapped her mouth shut, obviously unwilling to continue this discussion in
front of an audience. As George approached,
Stevie's mind raced, trying to take in what Carole
had said so far and balance it with what Lisa had
told her a few minutes earlier.

"Hi, Carole, Stevie." George stopped when he
reached the two girls and gave them one of his
typical shy smiles. He had started riding at Pine
Hollow a little over a year before when his family
had moved to Willow Creek. Stevie didn't know
him very well, even though he was a junior at
Fenton Hall and had been in a couple of her

classes the year before. But she knew enough to recognize that he was one of the best young riders at the stable, despite the fact that he didn't look like most people's idea of a rider. Because of his stocky, almost pudgy physique and his boyish, rounded face, it always seemed a little surprising that he could stay in the saddle at all, let alone that he had won countless ribbons in jumping and eventing.

But Stevie wasn't really thinking about any of that as she and Carole politely returned George's greeting. Stevie's mind drifted as George and Carole exchanged a few words about George's horse, a sleek gray Trakehner named Joyride. Stevie was still trying to make sense of the fight. When she had arrived, she had been certain Lisa was in the right and Carole in the wrong. But now . . .

Finally George moved on. As soon as he had disappeared at the end of the aisle, Carole turned back to Stevie. "Anyway," she said, "as I was saying, I was really torn up about keeping this from Lisa. But I figured she'd be even more worried if she knew the truth, and besides, I really didn't have any choice. She should have realized I have a responsibility to Max."

"Hmmm." Stevie leaned on the half door, thinking hard about what Carole had just said. "I think I get your point." She paused, trying to figure out how to phrase what she wanted to ask next. "Um, but did you consider talking to Max about this? You know, letting him know how upset Lisa was getting, maybe trying to convince him to let her in on the secret? You know she wouldn't have told anyone else."

Carole blinked. "What?"

Stevie gave her a close look. Was she imagining things, or were Carole's brown eyes just the slightest bit unfocused, as if her mind was wandering?

Stevie shook her head. This argument between her friends was making her paranoid. "You know, maybe you could have talked Max into telling her."

"Maybe." Carole shrugged. "But what if I had, and he'd said no? Lisa still would have jumped to conclusions and called me a liar and a bad friend." Her frown returned. "She didn't even give me a chance to explain. I know she was upset and everything, but it wasn't fair for her to take it out on me like that."

Stevie couldn't argue with that. "I guess," she said helplessly. "Um, but you aren't really going to hold that against her, are you?"

Carole just shrugged again, her face taking on a stubborn look. Stevie recognized that expression. It didn't turn up very often, but when it did it meant it wasn't going to be easy to change Carole's mind with anything short of a court order.

Stevie didn't know what to do. Carole had a

right to be mad. It sounded as though Lisa really had flown off the handle and said some hurtful, unfair things. Then again, she had only been reacting to what she considered a horrible betrayal of her friendship. Both of them might have gone overboard with their emotions, but neither was really wrong about what she was saying. How could either of them have acted any differently? But then again, how could two people who were supposedly best friends act that way toward each other at all? Stevie had no idea. The only thing that was clear in all this was that both her best friends were really angry with each other. She couldn't even begin to figure out how to fix that right now, especially since her mind was already so full of other problems. . . .

That reminded her of something. "Listen," she said. "Not to totally change the subject, but we're going to confront A.J. tomorrow afternoon. We're going to get all his friends together and challenge him to tell us what's bothering him these days. We want everyone to be at Phil's house by the time he gets home around four. Can you come?"

Carole looked wary. "I don't know. Is Lisa going to be there?"

"I hope so," Stevie replied frankly. "I forgot to mention it to her just now, but I'm going to call her as soon as I get home." She gave Carole a challenging look. "Why? Are you going to abandon A.J. just because you're mad at Lisa?"

For a moment, Carole's mulish expression deepened. But then a guilty, almost pained look passed like a shadow over her face, and she shook her head. "No, you're right," she said. "I'll be there—for A.J. I've got to stay after school for a little while, but I should be finished in time. And I'm sure Ben or Denise will cover for me here for an hour or two." She scowled. "But Lisa had better stay out of my way."

Stevie sighed. "Fine," she said shortly. "I'll see you tomorrow."

After Stevie left, Carole gave Starlight one last pat, then hurried down the aisle, feeling disgruntled. She was way behind schedule, thanks to all these interruptions, and she knew she had to get home soon if she wanted to have time to study for her makeup test. Why did Lisa have to pick today of all days to freak out? The clock was ticking, and Carole still had to finish grooming Samson. Besides that, she'd promised Red she would call the farrier and set up an appointment for several of the stable's horses before she left today, there was a pile of bandages waiting for her in the tack room—Red had washed them earlier, but Carole was supposed to roll them and put them away once they were dry—and someone had to bring down a few bales of hay from the loft.

She sped down the aisle and crossed the entry-way. The work wasn't going to do itself, so she might as well get started. Maybe she could roll the bandages while she was on the phone with the farrier . . .

When she rushed into the tack room, she found that it was already occupied. Three junior-high girls were there cleaning their tack. They had been chatting companionably with each other, but they fell silent as Carole entered the room, glancing at her curiously.

Carole suddenly realized that she must look like some kind of weird, unkempt mutant. She hadn't bothered to so much as glance at her hair after exercising Samson. If it was working true to form, she imagined that the dark curls that had lain beneath the rim of her hard hat were plastered to the side of her head by dried sweat. Meanwhile, the rest of her hair, which she had hurriedly plaited into a single long braid at the traffic lights between Willow Creek High School and the stable, was undoubtedly coming loose in huge, unruly clumps.

She forced herself to smile at the younger girls. "Hi, Juliet. May." She struggled to remember the name of the third girl, an occasional rider at best. "Um, Karen?"

"Katrina," the girl corrected.

"Sorry. Katrina." As Carole glanced around at

the three girls, a sudden feeling of intense, yearning nostalgia washed over her. These three friends could have been her, Stevie, and Lisa just a few years before. She couldn't remember how many times the three of them had sat in this very tack room, working and talking and holding endless meetings of The Saddle Club, a group they had formed soon after they'd all met.

Their lives had seemed so much simpler back then. So easy and full of fun. What had happened? When had things changed? She wasn't really sure. Maybe it had started when they had entered high school, with all its additional social and academic pressures. Or when Lisa's parents had divorced. Or even when Carole had switched from merely riding at Pine Hollow to working there as well.

But Carole was sure of one thing. Back in those days, Lisa never would have acted the way she'd acted today. She wouldn't have treated Carole that way. They had all changed in the past few years, but maybe Lisa had changed even more than Carole had realized. Maybe she wasn't the same person Carole had always known.

Suddenly the sound of May clearing her throat broke into her thoughts. Realizing that the three girls were staring at her questioningly—probably wondering why she was gazing at them with that sappy, wistful expression on her face—Carole felt herself blush.

Just then Katrina stood to return her bridle to its hook. That gave Carole an idea. "Listen, you three," she said briskly, doing her best to cover her lingering embarrassment. "I need to ask you to help me out here." She hurried over to the sink in the corner and dragged out the large bucket where she had stuffed the bandages earlier after bringing them in from the clothesline out back.

Out of the corner of her eye, she thought she caught Juliet rolling her eyes at Katrina. But she chose to ignore it.

"It looks like you're just about done here," she went on. "And someone needs to roll these clean bandages and stack them in the cabinet." She dropped the bucket at May's feet. "Guess what? You're elected."

Katrina groaned in protest, but May just sighed and set aside the girth she was cleaning. "Sure, Carole," she said. "We'll be happy to do it."

"Good." Carole stayed in the tack room just long enough to see each of the three girls get started on the bandages. She was pretty sure Max wouldn't mind what she had done. Yes, Carole had assured Red that *she* would take care of the bandages today. But as long as the job got done, what was the difference? Wasn't Max always talking about how every rider had to pitch in and help around the stable? Carole and her friends had certainly spent a good amount of time over the years rolling bandages, mucking out stalls, mixing feed, and doing all the other dull but necessary tasks that kept Pine Hollow running smoothly. Now it was these girls' turn to take over when Carole needed their help. It was good for them. It would help teach them not to take riding for granted.

Carole nodded, satisfied with her own argument. Then she hurried off toward the ladder to the hayloft.

Twenty minutes later, Carole slipped into Samson's stall. "I bet you thought I'd never come back, didn't you, handsome?" she murmured, raising her hands to the horse's finely sculpted head as he stepped forward to greet her. "Don't worry. I didn't forget I still owed you a good grooming."

She attached the nylon webbing across the front of the stall and reached for the grooming kit she had set in the aisle just outside. She had cooled Samson down and given him a quick rubdown after their training session that day, but she had put off a full grooming until she had time to do it properly. She didn't have quite as much time as she might have liked now, but there was nothing she could do about that. *Why is it that Ben never seems to be around when I really need him?* she thought peevishly. Red and Max had been busy with other things, so Carole had spent several valuable minutes searching for the young stable hand to help her bring down the hay. But Ben was nowhere to be found, and finally, feeling the minutes ticking away and imagining all those chapters waiting in her history book, Carole had given up and started hoisting bales herself. She had been almost finished when George Wheeler had happened by to lend a hand.

But none of that mattered now. As soon as she set eyes on Samson, Carole immediately felt one hundred percent better. After snapping a lead line to the big black horse's halter and attaching it to the ring on the wall—unlike many horses, Samson didn't need to be put in cross-ties when he was groomed—she ran her hand down his leg to ask him to lift his foot.

He did so promptly and she smiled, amazed as always at his eagerness to please her. "Thanks, fella," she said, hoisting a hoof pick and setting to work. "Don't worry, I'll have all four feet nice and clean before you know it."

Suddenly she paused, remembering that she had never called the farrier as she'd promised. Glancing at her watch, she saw that it was getting late.

The farrier is probably eating his dinner, she

thought. *Why bother him now? I can call him to-morrow. No big deal.*

She felt a moment of guilt as she reached the decision. But she shrugged it off. It wasn't that important. She returned her attention to Samson's hoof.

But for once, she felt her mind wandering as she tended to the big horse. Her fight with Lisa was really bothering her. What had made Lisa turn on her like that? It was still hard for Carole to believe some of the things Lisa had said.

"I can't believe I was so careful and excited about that whole stupid secret," she whispered to Samson, feeling rather sorry for herself. She had tried to do what was best for everyone, and look where it had gotten her. "I mean, not just the part about Prancer being pregnant, but the other stuff, too. . . ."

Her voice trailed off. She didn't really want to think about that right now. She wasn't even sure if Max had said anything to Lisa about the second part of Prancer's secret. What was more, she didn't really care. After the way Lisa had reacted, the last thing Carole wanted to think about was more surprises.

She blew out her lips in a loud sigh of frustration, wishing she could return to the good old days, when she could count on her friends to act the way they were supposed to. Why did people have to be so complicated?

"That's why I'm glad I have you, Samson," she murmured, lowering the foot she'd been working on and moving on to the next. "I can always count on you."

Samson snorted, seeming to agree with her comment, and Carole smiled. Pushing all her problems out of her head, she set to work on her grooming with renewed energy. If anything could make her forget her worries, it was spending some quality time with this brave, wonderful, loyal horse.

Later that night, Callie rolled over in her bed and glanced at Sheila, who was lying in a roll-away cot across the room. In the dim moonlight seeping into the room through the curtains, Sheila was little more than a dark shape against the sheets.

"So that's the rundown on Pine Hollow, I guess," Callie said. The girls had been talking since they'd turned out the lights an hour before. Actually, they'd been talking almost nonstop since that conversation in the backyard earlier in the day. Callie still couldn't get used to it, but she didn't want it to stop. Even the thought of sleep seemed like an unwelcome intrusion, an interruption of this strangely wonderful new intimacy.

"I wish I'd had a chance to visit the stable while I was here," Sheila said. "It sounds like a pretty cool place—probably even better than good old Greensprings Stable back home."

"Do you still go there much?"

"Not much," Sheila replied. "You know how it is—things are pretty busy right now. But seriously, do you think this Regnery guy is better or worse than your old trainer?"

Callie yawned as she considered the question. "Neither, really," she said thoughtfully. "Max isn't an endurance specialist or anything, but he really knows horses. I haven't thought about it that much." She laughed. "And now that I do think about it, that's kind of a surprise. I've spent an awful lot of time since we moved here comparing just about everything else to Valley Vista."

"Like what?"

"I don't know." Callie shrugged, though she knew Sheila probably couldn't see. "It's like I was saying earlier. Everything's so different, you know? The people, the weather, our house, the landscape . . ." She chuckled. "And then there's the accent, of course. I still haven't gotten used to that drawl a lot of people here have. It's like something from the movies."

Sheila laughed. "I don't know what y'all's talkin' 'bout," she drawled in an exaggerated Southern accent.

Callie giggled. And once she started, she couldn't seem to stop. It was only partly because Sheila had sounded so silly and mostly because Callie was feeling so happy and carefree and elated. She couldn't imagine what she had been so afraid of before. Why had she spent all those years closed in, keeping her thoughts and feelings to herself? In the course of a single day, all that had changed. She had shared things with Sheila that she had never told another soul—her thoughts, her fears and dreams, her unique view of the world. And nothing bad had happened. Why hadn't she tried it before?

"What are you laughing at?" Sheila asked, sounding perplexed.

Callie could hardly stop giggling long enough to respond. "Y'all!" she blurted out with some effort. Then she burst into fresh gales of helpless laughter.

This time Sheila joined in. The two of them shook and gasped with laughter, laughing so hard and long that Callie's stomach muscles started to ache. But she didn't care. It felt so good to let go like this. . . .

Eventually the girls' laughter died away. They lay still for a moment in the darkness, each thinking her own thoughts.

Sheila was the first to break the silence. "So what's the deal with this guy your friends kept talking about yesterday?" she asked. "I kept over-hearing all these weird little comments. What's his name—B.J. or something?"

"A.J.," Callie replied. Sheila's question reminded her about Stevie's phone call a few hours earlier. She had told Callie about the intervention and asked her to meet the others at Phil's house the next afternoon when she got back from taking Sheila to the airport. Callie felt a pang at the thought, and it had nothing to do with A.J.

I can't believe it, she told herself in amazement, her heart swelling with a strange mixture of joy and sadness. *A few days ago I was dreading the whole idea of Sheila's visit. And now I can hardly stand the thought that she has to leave!*

ELEVEN

Lisa hung back as the rest of her physics class stampeded for the doorway. The bell had just rung, releasing them from a confusing discussion of electromagnetism, and most of the students couldn't get away fast enough. But Lisa had been so distracted throughout the class that she'd barely heard a word anyone had said. She was still seething about what Carole had done. But more importantly, she was trying to figure out what the news about Prancer really meant.

She stepped into the hall, still moving slowly as she thought it all through one more time. The most difficult thing was figuring out how to feel about the whole situation. Part of her thought it was wonderful that Prancer might have the chance to pass on her sweet disposition and impressive athletic abilities to not one but two foals. But the larger part of her was filled with fear at what trying to bear twins might do to the beautiful Thoroughbred mare.

Of course, Lisa still felt rather surprised that Prancer had been bred at all—surprised and more than a little left out. Her rational mind knew very well that Prancer didn't belong to her. Max owned her in partnership with Judy Barker. The two of them had bought Prancer years earlier, after the accident that had ended her racing career. There was no reason they should consult Lisa or even inform her when they decided to breed their horse, even though Lisa had ridden Prancer more than anyone else over the years. She knew all that. But knowing it didn't stop her from feeling hurt at being left out of the loop.

I shouldn't be all that shocked that they decided to breed her, Lisa told herself as she made her way down the crowded school hallway. *If anything, I should be surprised they didn't do it before this. After all, Judy hasn't recouped much of her investment so far. That will only happen when Prancer starts having foals.*

Lisa shifted her books to her other arm and frowned. She was trying to be mature about this. But it wasn't easy to hold back the more immature, selfish, and chaotic thoughts that kept popping into her mind. Thoughts like *Why now? Why couldn't they have waited just one more year?*

She knew what this pregnancy meant. In most normal, uncomplicated pregnancies, a mare could be ridden up until around the fifth month of gestation. But in the case of twins, that sort of rule flew out the window. It was already obvious that Max didn't intend to let anyone ride Prancer anytime soon, and that meant she was sure to be off-limits throughout the rest of the eleven long months that she would carry her foals. By the time Prancer gave birth, Lisa would be graduating from high school. By the time her foals were weaned, Lisa would already be in her first semester at college.

It would have been hard enough for me to go away to school next fall and leave Prancer behind, she thought woefully. *It's not fair that I have to give her up a whole year early.*

She knew she wasn't being reasonable. It wasn't as though Prancer were really going anywhere. She would still be at Pine Hollow, where Lisa could visit her and spend time with her as often as she liked. But it wouldn't be the same, and Lisa knew it. Prancer wouldn't really belong to her anymore. There would be lots of other people looking after her, watching her, thinking and worrying and caring about her the way Lisa always had.

But not riding her. Nobody would be riding her. Lisa already missed the mare's spirited trot, her smooth, swift canter, the exhilarating feeling of crouching down as Prancer galloped faster than the wind. But now Prancer would be cooped up in her stall or in one of the smaller paddocks, taking it easy, for months and months to come.

Of course, that's if everything goes as it should. Lisa crossed her fingers, feeling fear trickle through her like cold water down her back. Her thoughts always came back to her fear—her terror that this pregnancy was too risky, that something awful would happen to Prancer or her foals. Prancer had never foaled before, and as if the risks of a plain old pregnancy weren't worrisome enough, the thought of twins was downright frightening.

Lisa sighed, trying to stop her endless, circling thoughts as she reached the doorway to the computer lab, where she had her next class. At that moment, she heard a commotion from the end of the hall.

Lisa turned to see what had happened. Carole was standing there, looking flustered as she stooped to pick up a whole pile of books and papers scattered at her feet. Lisa immediately guessed what had happened. Carole must have come barreling around the corner, late and disorganized as usual, and crashed into someone or something that had made her drop everything she was carrying.

For an instant, Lisa's instincts almost took over—she almost hurried forward to help Carole retrieve her things, as several other students were already doing. But then she remembered what had happened between them. Her face froze. *Let her clean up her own mess,* she thought contemptuously.

At that moment, Carole glanced up and met Lisa's eye. Lisa glared at her. Carole stared back stonily. A second later, Lisa tossed her head, turned away, and hurried into her classroom.

Carole was still annoyed about the encounter with Lisa when the final bell rang. *What's with her attitude, anyway?* she thought irritably.

But her anger turned to panic a moment later when she realized that the moment of truth had arrived. It was time to return to her history classroom and take that makeup test.

For a moment, Carole toyed with the idea of simply leaving, skipping the test. She could tell Ms. Shepard tomorrow that her father had had a relapse, that she couldn't take the test until next week . . .

But she knew that wouldn't work. She was lucky to have the chance to make up her poor grade at all; she didn't want to completely blow it.

Of course, I got a pretty good start on blowing it last night, she thought ruefully. *What was I thinking? I can't believe I lost track of the time like that.*

The evening before, Carole's quick grooming of Samson had turned into a long grooming. A very long grooming. It was already dark outside by the time she left Pine Hollow. And by the time she'd driven home, fixed herself a quick, solitary dinner of cereal and carrot sticks, and pulled out her books, her eyes were growing heavy. It had been a long, strenuous, emotionally draining day—first finding out she'd failed that stupid test, then the fight with Lisa, and of course Samson's intense training session and her sweating over those hay bales. She'd done her best to buckle down and read those chapters, but she had ended up falling asleep after little more than an hour, waking in the morning with her face in her textbook and her neck stiff.

She dragged her feet as she made her way down the hall toward Ms. Shepard's classroom, feeling like a prisoner walking to her own painful, undeserved execution. She had managed to get a little more reading done during her fourth-period study hall, but the cafeteria had been too noisy for her to study at lunch.

Now, as she walked, she pulled her history textbook out of her backpack and flipped it open, scanning the beginning of one of the chapters. But she was too nervous to concentrate properly, and the words blurred together in her mind, not making any sense. She paused in front of the classroom door, trying desperately to focus, to cram a last few bits of knowledge into her mind. She was startled by the sound of Ms. Shepard's voice greeting her.

"Ready for your retest, Carole?" the teacher asked cheerfully from just inside the classroom door. "Come on in and let's get started. I don't want to keep you any longer than I have to."

Carole gulped. "I'm coming." She shoved the textbook back into her bag and stepped across the threshold with a heavy heart.

"Carole," Ms. Shepard said half an hour later.

Carole blinked and looked up. The teacher was sitting at her desk at the front of the room, where she had been correcting papers while Carole struggled with the retest. "Yes? My time isn't up yet, is it?"

Ms. Shepard laughed. "No, no, don't worry," she said. "You still have plenty of time. I just wanted to tell you that I have to go down to the office to use the photocopier. But I'll be back in ten minutes or so in case you have any questions. All right?"

Carole nodded dumbly, relieved and disappointed at the same time. She was relieved because she still hadn't managed to come up with answers to more than a third of the test questions, even though there was a smaller proportion of essay questions this time around. The disappointment sprang from her conviction that she could sit at her desk until clocks ran backward and a pig won the Kentucky Derby and she still wouldn't know the answers. At least if her time were up this nightmare would be over.

The teacher gathered some papers and left the room, and the sound of her heels tapping against the hard tile floor grew fainter and fainter. Left alone in the classroom, Carole tapped her pencil on her desk nervously. Tears of frustration sprang to her eyes as she scanned the questions once more. There was no way out of this—no way she could pass this test today, no way she would be able to convince Ms. Shepard to let her try a third time.

You know what that means, Carole told herself, feeling her heart constrict at the thought. *That means no more Pine Hollow for at least a month.* She had already estimated that it would take that long to bring up her average if she failed again.

The idea was almost too horrible to bear. Carole had never lost her riding privileges before, and she couldn't even imagine what it would be like. Max would be terribly disappointed in her, and her father would probably have a fit when he got home from his trip and found out about it. How could she have let this happen?

She didn't really know the answer to that. Her life had been so busy lately, so complicated. But that wasn't really important. What was important now was that she had messed up, big-time, and there didn't seem to be any way out. She was trapped in this disaster, and she would have to find a way to deal with it.

Carole dropped her pencil, swiveled sideways in her chair to stretch out her legs, and rubbed her forehead with both hands, as if by doing so she could force the right answers into her mind. She squeezed her eyes shut.

When she opened them a few seconds later, she found herself staring at her own legs—and her backpack, which she had dropped on the floor beside her desk. The top zipper was partway open, and Carole could see the edge of her red-white-and-blue history textbook poking out of the opening.

She blinked. *All the answers I need are right in there,* she thought. *All in that book, in black and white.*

She gulped and glanced around the empty room, feeling guilty for even thinking such a thing. Her teacher had trusted her enough to leave her alone in the room. How could she even entertain the thought of breaching that trust?

I'm no cheater, she told herself sternly. That was true enough. But her eyes strayed back to her backpack, sitting there so temptingly close. She dragged her gaze back to the desktop, feeling uncomfortable. She wished Ms. Shepard would hurry up and return so that she could stop thinking this way.

She picked up her pencil again and held it so tightly her knuckles paled. Grabbing her test paper, she read through the first few questions once more, willing her brain to come up with the right answers.

But that was hopeless. Carole didn't know the answers. She counted up the number of questions she had answered and did some quick mental calculations. The answer made her cringe. Even in the unlikely event that she received full credit for every response she had come up with so far, she would still fall at least fifteen points short of any kind of passing grade.

Her heart started to pound even before she was consciously aware of what she was about to do. After a quick glance at the open classroom door, she leaned over and grabbed the textbook out of her bag. Her heart in her throat, she quickly flipped it open to the section covered by the test.

It was almost too easy. The answers she needed seemed to leap out at her from the text, begging to be used. Carole started scribbling frantically, keeping one ear tuned to the doorway. By the time she heard the faint click, click of Ms. Shepard's high heels drifting down the hall, she had found most of the answers she needed.

She closed the book and stuffed it back in her

bag, shoving the whole thing out of sight beneath her chair seconds before her smiling teacher reentered the room. Fearing that her face would give away what she had done, she bent over her paper, writing busily.

"I'm back, Carole," Ms. Shepard announced cheerfully. "How's it going?"

Carole kept her eyes on her paper. "Fine," she said, doing her best to sound normal. "Um, I think I'm almost finished."

"Good, good." The teacher turned away and busied herself at her desk, humming under her breath.

Carole took a few deep breaths of her own. She had to get a grip. If Ms. Shepard guessed what she had done . . . But she wouldn't guess. Carole would make sure of that. She let a few more minutes pass, then got up and turned in her paper. Ms. Shepard looked pleased as she glanced over the first few questions.

Carole grabbed her backpack and scurried out of the room. Her heart rate had almost returned to normal, but she still couldn't believe what she had just done. Still, she hadn't had any choice, had she? If she hadn't looked up those answers, she never could have passed. She would have been banned from Pine Hollow, where so many people and horses were counting on her. How could she have left Ben and Red and Denise and the rest of the staff with extra work in her absence? How could she take care of Starlight properly if she couldn't even ride him? Most importantly, how could she ever have forgiven herself for abandoning Samson at such a critical point in his training? She was starting to suspect that Max might consider entering the big black horse in the prestigious Colesford Horse Show, and she couldn't bear the thought that his chances could be ruined by one stupid test.

She still felt queasy as she stepped outside. Pausing on the school steps, she took a long, deep breath of the warm early-October air. She wasn't sure, but she thought she detected a hint of coolness in the mild breeze that tousled her hair as she stood there. It was starting to feel like autumn, a season that always reminded her of pleasant things—the sound of hooves on crisp fallen leaves, snuggling down in scratchy straw during hayrides, the warm smell of a healthy horse in a cozy stall.

She had done what she had to do. There was no point in dwelling on it any longer. With that, Carole put the whole incident out of her mind and hurried toward the student parking lot. She had promised Emily she would pick her up at Pine Hollow on her way to Phil's house. If she hurried, she could swing by Samson's stall for a few minutes before they had to leave.

TWELVE

Stevie hurried up the walkway toward the Marstens' front door. Scott and Alex were right behind her.

"I hope he's not here yet," Stevie muttered, gazing anxiously at the old stone house as she approached. She glanced back at the two guys. "I never knew you drove like such a senior citizen, Scott. I thought we'd never get here."

Alex snorted, and Scott smiled uncertainly. "Don't worry, Stevie," he said. "It's not like a surprise party. It doesn't really matter if everyone beats A.J. here. After all, Callie's definitely going to be late." He glanced at his watch. "She and Dad and Sheila must be about halfway to the airport by now."

Stevie didn't bother to respond. The three of them had reached the door, and she reached up and rapped sharply with the horseshoe-shaped brass knocker.

Phil opened the door almost immediately.

A.J.'s ex-girlfriend, Julianna, a petite redhead who went to Cross County High School with Phil and A.J., was standing just behind him, her face pale.

"Bad news," Phil said dejectedly. "He's not coming."

Stevie gasped. "What? What happened?"

Phil stood aside and gestured wearily for them to enter. Once they were all inside, he closed the door with a thud and led them toward the living room. "He told me in last period today," he explained, flopping down into his favorite easy chair. "Said he has a dentist's appointment he forgot about."

"He's probably lying," Julianna put in, her voice angry. "He probably just decided he didn't want to see anyone, so he made up that story."

Stevie glanced at her. For a moment, in her disappointment over Phil's news, she had almost forgotten that the other girl was present. Julianna was the kind of girl Stevie would never have bothered to get to know if she hadn't been A.J.'s girlfriend. In fact, Stevie had never quite understood what A.J. saw in her. To give credit where credit was due, Stevie would have admitted that Julianna was lively and easy to talk to, with enough sense to laugh when something was funny. And there was no denying that she was pretty, with all the qualities that made teenage boys drool. Stevie didn't really mind having Julianna around, but she didn't especially enjoy her company, either. There was something a little too careless, a bit shallow even, in her personality that had kept Stevie and most of A.J.'s other friends from warming up to her.

Still, Stevie had developed a greater appreciation for Julianna once she'd realized that she really cared about A.J. and was hurt by the breakup. She gave her a sympathetic glance before perching on the arm of Phil's chair. "So what do we do now?"

Scott shrugged. "What can we do? We can't go chain him up and drag him over here."

"Are you sure about that?" Stevie asked, only half joking.

The sound of the knocker interrupted the conversation. Phil hurried toward the door and returned a moment later with Carole and Emily.

"Did you hear?" Stevie asked them gloomily.

Emily nodded. "Bummer," she said, lowering herself carefully onto the couch and resting her arms on her crutches. "So what now?"

Stevie glanced around at each of the six other people in the room. She didn't have an answer, and from the looks of things, neither did anyone else. Phil had sunk back into his chair, his face set and grim. Scott was staring out the window, his brow deeply furrowed. Alex and Emily looked worried and thoughtful. Carole was chewing on her lower lip, her eyes distant. Julianna was clearly on the verge of tears, wavering somewhere between frustration and sadness.

Before long, the sound of the knocker came again. "That must be Lisa," Stevie said.

"I'll get it," Scott volunteered, already moving toward the door.

Stevie glanced up when Lisa entered the room. She could tell by the look on her face that Scott had filled her in.

"Sorry this didn't work out, Phil, Stevie," Lisa said softly, making a beeline for Alex's side and wrapping her arm around his waist. "It was a good idea." She glanced around the room. "Hello, everyone. It's good to see you, Emily. You too, Julianna. Scott, did Callie get Sheila off to the airport okay?"

"They're on their way now," Stevie answered for him, feeling decidedly uncomfortable. She couldn't help noticing that Lisa had addressed everyone in the room by name except for Carole. When Stevie glanced at Carole, she saw that she had clearly noticed the same thing, judging by the dark scowl on her face.

"So what are we going to do?" Lisa asked, addressing herself to Phil.

Phil shrugged. "I guess there's not much we can do today," he said heavily. "We'll have to try again. Maybe later in the week."

"In that case, I'd better get going," Carole said

quickly. "I should get back to Pine Hollow and get to work." She took a few steps toward the door. "Emily, can you find another ride home?"

"I can drop her off," Julianna volunteered. "I'm staying at my dad's house tonight, and he lives on the other side of Willow Creek. Right near your place," she added, glancing at Emily.

"Thanks," Emily said. "See you, Carole. Don't work too hard."

"Bye, Emily." Carole smiled at her. She turned toward Phil and Stevie. "See you later, Phil. You too, Stevie. Keep your spirits up, Julianna." She fished her car keys out of her pocket as she continued toward the door. "Bye, Scott. Tell Callie I'm sorry I missed her. Later, Alex."

With that, she hurried out of the room. Stevie ran one hand through her hair, feeling dismayed. She hadn't thought much more about her friends' big fight, assuming that Carole and Lisa would have gotten over their anger by now. But they had both just proved, rather childishly, that they hadn't.

Since there didn't seem to be much she could do about A.J.'s problems at the moment, she decided to tackle this one instead. She stood and walked over to where Lisa and Alex were standing near the doorway as Julianna drifted toward Emily and Scott started talking to Phil.

"Hi," she greeted Lisa. "Um, how's it going?"

Lisa leaned back into Alex's shoulder. "It's going," she replied shortly.

Stevie hesitated. Then she shrugged and plunged right in. "So I guess this means you're still mad at Carole, huh?"

"Oops!" Alex dropped his arm from around Lisa's shoulders and held up both hands in a position of surrender. "This sounds like my cue to leave." He hurried away toward the other guys, leaving Stevie and Lisa alone.

Lisa didn't look happy about his departure. "Look," she told Stevie with a frown. "If you're here to try to talk me into making up with *her*"— she grimaced slightly—"you might as well save your breath. It's not going to happen."

"But listen," Stevie urged. "If you think about it, this is all just a big mix-up. It's nobody's fault, really."

Lisa let out a sharp, incredulous laugh. "How can you say that!" she exclaimed. "You know what she did. The more I think about it, the madder I get. I mean, we've all been friends too long to start keeping secrets like that." She crossed her arms over her chest, her face set and angry. "It's all her fault."

Stevie sighed. "Whatever," she muttered, feeling a little annoyed herself. How could she help her friends work through this when they were both being so immature about it? *First Carole*

213

rushes off like she'll be poisoned if she breathes the same air as Lisa for more than twenty seconds, she thought bitterly. *Now Lisa is acting like some sulky little girl who's pouting because someone accidentally broke her favorite toy.*

She mumbled some kind of excuse and wandered back toward Phil's chair. He was talking to Scott, but he looked up and reached for her as she approached. She took his hand and perched once more on the wide, overstuffed arm of the chair.

"I guess there's no point in everyone sticking around," he said, rubbing the back of her hand with his thumb.

Stevie squeezed his hand. She had just been thinking the same thing. In fact, she was starting to wish that everyone else would hurry up and leave. Phil could use some cheering up, and so could she. They would have better luck improving each other's mood by spending some quality time alone, preferably snuggled deep into the cushions of the couch.

"I hope you're not trying to get rid of everyone," Scott told Phil with a casual smile. "Because you're stuck with me for a while. Dad's planning to drop Callie off here on his way from the airport to some meeting over in Berryville, so I've got to wait for her or she'll be stranded here." He shrugged. "Maybe we can shoot some hoops or something while we wait."

214

For a moment Stevie felt disappointed. But then she thought better of it. *Phil misses the old A.J. more than any of us,* she thought. *After all, they've been best friends forever. Maybe what he really needs right now is another guy friend to hang out with. It's nice that Scott is here for him—I should let them have some time alone.*

She smiled, feeling pleased at her sudden insight and rather noble at her determination to encourage this male bonding. "You two have fun," she told Phil and Scott. "I'd better hop a ride home with Lisa. My English teacher assigned about a million pages of reading today, and I'm going to be up until midnight as it is."

"Okay." Phil leaned forward to give her a kiss. "I'll call you later."

In a few minutes Stevie had shepherded Alex and Lisa outside to Lisa's car. Emily and Julianna had just waved good-bye and taken off in Julianna's car, and Scott and Phil were still inside.

"Well, that was a total bust," Alex announced as he walked around to the passenger side and tilted the seat forward.

Stevie stepped past him and hopped into the backseat. "Tell me about it," she mumbled as Lisa turned the key in the ignition. "I can't believe he blew it off."

That wasn't really true. She *did* believe it. The

way A.J. was acting these days, she would have believed just about any negative thing he did.

Lisa carefully backed down Phil's driveway, which opened onto a quiet country road with only a few other houses in sight. "Well, it wasn't actually a total waste," she said lightly. "After all, any time I get to be with my baby can't be all bad." She glanced over at Alex and blew him a kiss.

Alex scooted as close to her as his seat belt and the car's bucket seats would allow. "No way," he cooed. "Even a trip to the dentist would be like a dream come true if my gorgeous little sweetie was there with me." He reached over and rubbed her knee. "I wouldn't even need any Novocain if I could just look into your eyes."

Stevie rolled her eyes. She hated it when Alex and Lisa got like this. Fortunately it didn't happen too often. But once they got started it was hard to stop them. "Keep your eyes on the road," she snapped irritably as Lisa glanced over at Alex again and giggled.

Lisa didn't even seem to hear her. She took her right hand off the steering wheel, reached over, and ran her fingers lightly through Alex's hair. "Did anyone ever tell you you're probably the nicest, sweetest guy ever to live?"

Stevie groaned. "I'm trapped in flirting hell,"

she muttered, not even expecting to be heard by the lovebirds in the front seat.

She stared out the window at the trees, fields, and houses they were passing, doing her best to ignore the nauseating flirtation still going on in the front seat. It was hard to believe that someone as sensible and no-nonsense as Lisa could sound like such a doofus. People could really surprise you when they fell in love. Still, this time at least, Stevie suspected that there might be a reason for Lisa's behavior—a reason that had nothing to do with Alex. Lisa was probably trying to take her mind off her problems with Carole. Underneath that practical exterior, Lisa could be awfully sensitive, and that meant that when someone hurt her, she felt it deeply. Maybe she had overreacted a little to that whole business with Prancer, but no matter what she said now, she had to be upset that she and Carole weren't speaking. Stevie couldn't really blame her for trying to take her mind off that.

Still, as she listened to the couple's silly baby talk, Stevie couldn't help wondering about something else. Until this moment she had forgotten all about her chat with Lisa in the ladies' room of the restaurant on Saturday night. But now it all came back to her. And from the look and sound of things, she strongly suspected that Lisa still hadn't had that little talk with Alex as she had promised.

Isn't she ever going to tell him that she almost stayed in California? she wondered anxiously. *Alex deserves to know the truth. He shouldn't be kept in the dark about something so important.*

She tapped her fingers on the seat beside her, trying to figure out what to do about this. What more *could* she do? She'd already told Lisa what she thought about the whole situation, although it didn't seem to have made much of a difference.

Maybe I should just tell him myself, she thought. *After all, he is my twin brother, and Lisa can't really expect me to keep this kind of secret from him. . . .*

The thought trailed off as Stevie's mind flashed back to her friends' fight. Carole had kept an important secret from Lisa, and look where that had gotten them both. Then again, she realized, Carole had only kept that secret because someone else she cared about—Max—had asked her to, just the way Lisa had asked Stevie to keep quiet about her decision.

But what did that mean? It seemed to mean that if Stevie told Alex what she knew, she was taking sides *with* Lisa at the same time she was acting *against* her wishes. It would be like agreeing that she was right in thinking that Carole should have told Lisa about Prancer, because she would be making the point that Lisa should have told Alex about the California decision.

Stevie shook her head, feeling confused. She liked to consider herself an honest, fair person, but sometimes it was hard to know what that meant.

She glanced forward as Lisa let out another giggle. Stevie was sitting behind the driver's seat, so she couldn't see much of Lisa other than the back of her head. But she had a good view of her brother's face as he gazed lovingly at his girlfriend. Alex had that look in his eyes that he only got when he was with Lisa, a look that always made Stevie feel a warm, selfless glow deep inside her. Her twin was truly happy, truly in love. How could she jeopardize that by telling him Lisa's secret? It would break his heart. Not to mention what it would do to her own relationship with her friend.

Stevie leaned back and closed her eyes. She had reached a decision. This whole issue was none of her business. *Yes, Alex is my brother,* she thought, *and yes, Lisa's my best friend. But they're also a couple, and they have to work this one out between themselves. Even if I think Alex should know the whole truth about this, it's not my place to tell him Lisa's secret.*

She opened her eyes and stared out the window again at the peaceful scenery rolling by. But she hardly saw any of it. She still wasn't quite sure whether she was doing what was absolutely best for everyone by keeping quiet. But she was sure about one thing: Lisa would never intentionally hurt Alex. And that was really all that mattered.

Carole barely waited for her battered old car to come to its usual shuddering stop before she was out the door and hurrying toward the stable. She'd already pushed aside all unpleasant thoughts of Lisa and A.J. and was simply looking forward to a nice long workout with Samson.

The wide double main doors were standing open, letting in the last rays of late-afternoon sunshine. Carole strode through them, blinking hard as her eyes worked to adjust to the relative dimness within.

"Carole."

Carole jumped and blinked again, willing her pupils to start working. She turned and squinted at the figure who had just stepped out of the tack room hallway. "Huh? Oh, hi, Ben. I didn't see you there."

Ben didn't answer for a moment. He stepped forward, both hands shoved deep in the pockets of his worn, faded jeans.

Carole's eyes were finally behaving, and she could see Ben's face well enough to tell that he was frowning. That was no big surprise—Ben was one of the most serious people she knew. He never seemed to be able to lighten up and let his guard down with people. The only creatures he really trusted were horses. With them, Ben was caring, generous, and kind. Most people found that odd, but Carole understood perfectly. She just wished Ben could open up a little more with people, too—at least with the people who wanted to be his friends.

She didn't have time to try to figure him out at the moment, though. The days were getting shorter, and she would have to hurry if she wanted to take Samson outside for any decent length of time. She was planning to do some flatwork in the big west field, where there wouldn't be any distractions. "Did you need something, Ben?" she asked, trying to hide her impatience.

"Uh, not really." Ben glanced down at his feet, rocking back on the heels of his dusty work boots. "I just—well."

Carole bit back a frustrated sigh. Ben could be pretty tongue-tied around a lot of people, but he usually managed to speak in complete sentences when he was talking to her. What was his problem? She didn't really care right now. "Okay, then," she said lightly. "Well, I'd better go see if Samson—"

"Samson." Ben blurted out that single word,

then cleared his throat. "Er, I wanted to talk to you about Samson."

That piqued Carole's interest. "What about him?"

Ben shrugged. "Well, I was noticing. I mean, you've been spending a lot of time with him. A lot. You've got other jobs here, and . . ."

His voice trailed off again, and Carole frowned. What was he driving at? Out of the blue, an image of her history textbook popped into her mind, but she pushed it aside. "If you've got some kind of complaint about my work, why don't you just say so?" she told Ben a bit testily.

"No, no." Ben took his hands out of his pockets and ran them through his thick, dark hair. He glanced around aimlessly as if searching for the right words. "It's just, well, Samson. I've noticed—he's not really your horse or anything, and you—"

"Whatever." Carole cut him off brusquely. She'd had enough of Ben's pointless hemming and hawing. Suddenly she guessed what might be upsetting him. "Listen, I know you wanted to help me train Samson when he first came back, and I'm sorry I said no. But I just think a horse like him is better off learning from one person. I hope you understand." She set her chin and hurried forward toward the hallway to the tack room, her eyes daring Ben to stand in her way.

He stepped aside, his dark eyes impossible to read. "I understand," he said as she brushed past him, his voice so low that she wasn't sure she'd heard him right. "Perfectly."

THIRTEEN

The next morning, Carole yawned as she stood at the counter pouring herself a glass of orange juice. "Want some, Dad?" she asked sleepily.

Colonel Hanson glanced up from his seat at the small round table by the kitchen window and smiled. "No thanks, sweetie." He held up his mug. "Coffee's all I want right now."

Carole smiled back. It was good to have her father home again. His trip had only lasted a week, but it had seemed much longer. "No wonder," she said. "You got in so late last night I thought it might all be a dream."

"No such luck," Colonel Hanson joked, taking a sip of coffee. "I'm back, and I don't have any other speaking engagements scheduled for the rest of the month. So I'm afraid you'll have to put a stop to all those wild parties I'm sure you've been throwing every night."

Carole laughed weakly. She had never even considered having a party while her father was away—how would she find the time?—but she couldn't block a twinge of guilt when she thought about her grades.

She shook her mind to get rid of the thought. Taking her glass, she sat down opposite her father. "How did your speeches go?"

"Oh, just fine." Colonel Hanson chuckled. "At this point I've given that speech on commitment and honor in the business world so many times I could do it in my sleep. You might as well call me Colonel Robot."

Carole smiled, feeling a flash of pride. Her father was being modest—Carole knew he had been in great demand ever since he'd retired from the Marine Corps and started taking on these motivational speaking engagements. He had also expanded his volunteer role in several charities and other nonprofit agencies. Colonel Hanson had always been every inch the good Marine, but unlike some members of the military, he never forgot to be human as well. He had a quick sense of humor and a warm, likable manner that came across in his every word and action. *It's no wonder people are lining up to hear what he has to say,* Carole thought fondly.

"But enough of my trip," Colonel Hanson went on, setting down his mug. "What have you been up to this past week?" His deep brown eyes

225

twinkled. "You haven't by any chance been spending time at the stable, have you?"

Carole grinned. "How'd you guess?" she said. "Seriously, though, this week was great. Samson seems to get stronger every day that I train him. Just yesterday, we were working on some turns, and—"

"Samson?" Colonel Hanson interrupted, furrowing his brow. "Wait, don't tell me. Is that one of Max's new horses?"

Carole frowned slightly. She was sure she had told her father all about Samson's training before this. "That's right," she said, doing her best to be patient. After all, he hadn't had much sleep the night before. "He's the one who was born at Pine Hollow, remember? Stevie and—um, my friends and I assisted in his birth. The big black horse."

"Oh, right." Colonel Hanson laughed. "Of course. You told me all about him last month. Sorry, I guess I'm a little fuzzy this morning." He gulped down the rest of his coffee and rose to get more from the pot on the counter. "So how's good old Starlight?"

"He's fine." Carole shrugged. "Same as always. So anyway, like I was saying, Samson's getting so good that it's almost scary. I'm hoping Max will want to enter him in a show soon—you know, sort of test him out." She grinned and crossed her fingers, holding them up so that her father could see. "Since I'm working so hard training him, I'm hoping if he does, he'll let me ride him. I'm pretty sure he will. I mean, I do know Samson better than anyone else."

Colonel Hanson blew on his steaming coffee mug as he sat down. "Is that right?" He gave Carole a curious glance. "Well, I guess you have been busy. I hope in between all this training you remembered to go to school."

"Very funny." Carole forced a laugh, once again squelching the unwelcome memory of that history test. "School's fine. Same as always."

"And how are Lisa and Stevie doing? I haven't seen either of them in ages."

"They're fine." Carole kept her voice neutral. She didn't want him to know about her fight with Lisa. She wasn't quite sure why—she and her father had been very close ever since Carole's mother had died five years earlier, and she had long made a habit of confiding in him about all sorts of problems. But this fight was different from the silly little arguments she'd had with her friends in the past, and she wasn't sure her father would understand. He would probably just try to talk her out of being angry with Lisa, to convince her to find a way to reconcile their differences, and Carole wasn't sure she wanted that. She wasn't sure she wanted to forgive Lisa so easily for the hurtful things she'd said.

227

Colonel Hanson shrugged. "Well, that's good. How about the folks at the stable? That nice young fellow, Ben—I hope he hasn't given up on his plans for college."

Carole winced, wishing for a split second that she'd never told her father about all that. Ben had hoped to win a scholarship to enroll in an equine studies program at a local university, but that had fallen through, and he hadn't mentioned college since.

"I'm not sure, Dad," she said, remembering Ben's weird comments about Samson the afternoon before at the stable. What had that been all about? Ben was usually the last person to poke his nose into other people's business. He was so intensely private that Carole had assumed he respected other people's privacy as well. So why was he bugging her about Samson all of a sudden? "I guess Ben's fine. Everybody's fine." She forced a laugh. "I mean, you were only gone a week. It's not like anything very exciting could happen around here in that amount of time." She glanced at her watch. "I'd better get ready to go, or I'll be late for school."

Lisa stared at her copy of *The Canterbury Tales*, which was lying on the desk in front of her, open to the middle of "The Miller's Tale." All around her, her classmates were laughing at something

228

her English teacher had just said. In fact, most of the students had been cracking up throughout the class. But Lisa wasn't finding the discussion very amusing.

"All right, then." Ms. Thorpe raised her hands for quiet. "I think we all agree that the carpenter comes out looking quite the fool in this tale. What do you think the other pilgrims would have thought about him after listening to the miller's story?"

Lisa didn't pay much attention to her classmates' responses. *They probably thought the carpenter's wife was a real jerk,* she thought glumly. Unlike the other students, Lisa didn't see much to laugh at in the bawdy tale, despite its references to farting and fondling and other silly things. Once you got past that stuff, and fought your way through all that obtuse Middle English language, it was really just a story of a dishonest, unfaithful wife pulling the wool over the eyes of her innocent, deluded husband. And that particular theme struck straight at Lisa's conscience these days.

She squirmed uncomfortably in her seat, wishing the class would end so that she could stop thinking about this. She already felt guilty enough about not following through on her promise to Stevie. But ignoring the problem wouldn't make it go away, and she had put off the subject long enough already.

I've got to find a way to tell Alex the truth, she thought. *But I have to do it so he'll understand.*

She chewed on her lower lip, trying to imagine how she could find the words to explain it to him. It shouldn't be so difficult—wasn't his almost uncanny ability to understand her one of the things she loved best about him?

But this confession would be a different kind of test for their relationship, a scary one from Lisa's point of view because for once she wasn't sure he would understand. *How would I feel if I were him?* she wondered, not for the first time. *Would I stop loving him if he considered leaving me behind to try new things?*

Her heart ached at the very thought. She couldn't imagine that she would ever stop loving Alex for any reason. She couldn't imagine her life without his caring, supportive, wonderful presence in it.

Then again, a little voice inside her said, *you never could have imagined hating one of your best friends, could you?*

Tears sprang to Lisa's eyes before she could stop them. She quickly lowered her gaze to her book, hoping no one would notice. Luckily, the other students were distracted by a lively discussion that seemed to have something to do with body odor and bathing.

Lisa blinked hard and took a few deep, quiet

breaths, trying to get her emotions back under control. She was still angry at Carole—so angry that it sometimes made her hands start to shake involuntarily. But she was also deeply hurt at her friend's betrayal. How could this have happened? They had always been so close that it was hard to believe they were now so deeply divided.

She rubbed her face wearily, feeling drained. Promise or no promise, any decision—any action—regarding Alex would have to wait. It was just too much to deal with right now when she had so many other things on her mind. First she had to figure out how to come to terms with Prancer's condition and how to make peace with her own hostile feelings toward Carole. She couldn't stand the thought of a confrontation with Alex until those issues were out of the way.

Stevie was standing in front of her gym locker rubbing her face with a towel when she heard the familiar soft taps of Callie's crutches behind her. She tossed the towel into the jumble of clothes and shoes at the bottom of the locker and slammed the metal door shut. Then she turned to smile at Callie.

"Hi," she said. "What did George want?"

Callie shrugged and lowered herself onto the slatted bench in front of the row of lockers.

231

"Nothing important," she reported. "He just had a question about our chem assignment."

Stevie did her best not to smirk and give away her own thoughts. She wasn't always the most observant person in the world where others' feelings were concerned, but she had the sneaking suspicion that George Wheeler had developed a little crush on Callie. Callie didn't seem to have noticed, though, and since Stevie seriously doubted she could ever have any romantic interest in a chubby, nerdy guy like George—no matter how good a rider he was—she didn't plan to breathe a word.

"Anyway," she said, sitting down beside Callie on the bench, "I was hoping we'd still be doing those physical fitness tests today so we'd have a chance to talk." Stevie hadn't seen Callie since Sheila had left, and she was dying for a full report. She rolled her eyes. "Leave it to Ms. Monroe to decide she's in the mood for dodgeball."

Callie laughed. "I don't know," she teased. "You seemed to be pretty into it." She glanced around at the other girls who were busily changing clothes, putting on makeup, and chatting all around them. "Actually, though, I was hoping to talk to you, too." Her eyes sparkled. "I wanted to thank you again for helping me realize that Sheila and I—that our relationship could be different than it was. I never would have been able to do it

232

without you. I never would have *thought* to do it without you."

Stevie smiled back at Callie, pleased. Even the fact that Callie was being so honest and direct about her feelings right then was proof that she was learning to open up more, let herself be vulnerable. "I didn't do that much," Stevie protested modestly. "You did all the hard work."

"It *was* hard," Callie admitted. "But most things that are worth anything are hard, and this one was definitely worth it." She shrugged. "I mean, I'm still not sure Sheila and I will ever be as close as you and Carole and Lisa are, but . . ."

Stevie didn't really hear what Callie said right after that. She winced at the mention of her two best friends. These days, Stevie wasn't sure that she and Carole and Lisa should be held up as any great example of friendship.

Especially Carole and Lisa, she thought rather sourly. She still couldn't believe that a relatively minor disagreement—in her opinion, anyway—had blown up into such a huge deal. She never would have expected it, never would have guessed that two people she thought she knew so well would react this way.

She did her best to shrug off the thought, not wanting her other friends' fight to intrude on her happiness for Callie. Whatever was wrong between Carole and Lisa, it had nothing to do with Callie and Sheila.

Ms. Shepard was waiting in the hall outside her classroom when Carole reached it that afternoon. As soon as she saw the teacher, Carole's heart started to pound. Part of her had been dreading this moment, fearing that what she had done had all been for nothing, that she had failed the test anyway. But another part was glad it was finally here. Now she would find out her fate, and she could begin putting this whole unpleasant incident behind her.

The teacher smiled when she spotted her. "Oh, there you are, Carole," she said, holding up something that could only be the test, though it was turned away from her. "I was waiting for you—I didn't want to keep you in suspense any longer than necessary."

Carole numbly reached for the paper as her teacher handed it to her. A quick glance was all it took to send relief flooding through her, so strong and sudden that her knees felt weak. At the top of the first page, in bold red ink, was the letter B. She had passed, and then some. Her riding privileges were safe once again.

"Thanks, Ms. Shepard," she said earnestly. "I really appreciate your letting me retake the test."

You'll never know quite how much, she added

silently, an image of Samson floating through her mind as she scurried past the teacher into the classroom. As soon as she was inside she stuffed the test into her backpack, way deep down to the bottom, never wanting to look at it again.

"Can you feel them in there yet?" Lisa murmured, running her hand over Prancer's glossy flank. "I can't. But you must know you're going to be a mommy. Don't you?"

The mare gazed back at her placidly, chewing a mouthful of hay. Her large, liquid eyes held no answers, and Lisa sighed.

She was doing her best to get used to the idea of twin foals growing inside Prancer. That was hard enough, since the mare hadn't begun to show yet. Even more difficult to accept was the fact that Lisa wasn't going to be able to ride Prancer for the foreseeable future. She had thought she'd had it tough before, not knowing when the mare would be back in service. But now that she knew the truth, it was almost worse. Now Lisa knew for a fact that she wouldn't get to ride Prancer for well over a year, if ever.

"It makes the whole idea of riding seem a lot less fun all of a sudden," she whispered to Prancer, feeling very sorry for herself. "If I can't ride you, maybe I shouldn't bother to ride at all anymore. At least not quite so often," she added quickly. The thought of giving up riding entirely was rather extreme. But maybe it was time to think about doing other things.

Something made her glance toward the stall door at that moment, and she almost jumped out of her skin when she saw Ben Marlow standing outside watching her. "How long have you been standing there?" she snapped, blushing at the thought that he might have overheard her heartfelt whispers to the pregnant horse.

"Not long," Ben replied. "I was looking for you. Red said he saw you come in."

Lisa gave Prancer one last pat and moved to the front of the stall, carefully keeping her gaze averted from Ben's as she let herself out of the stall. The guy made her a little nervous at the best of times—she could never guess what he was thinking behind that brooding expression—and he had startled her badly just now, making her feel rather skittish. "Well, you found me," she said as calmly as she could. "What's up?"

Ben shrugged, looking uncomfortable. "I thought I should talk to you," he said hesitantly. "Um, I've noticed some things lately. Things about Carole, and I thought you . . . well . . ."

Lisa could hardly believe her ears. Since when did loner Ben start getting involved in other people's personal business? And why had he decided to start with hers? "I see where you're going with this," she blurted out before she could stop herself. "And it's none of your business."

Ben seemed taken aback. "But I just wanted—I know you two—ah, never mind." He scowled, obviously regretting ever starting this conversation. "See you." He spun on his heel and stalked off down the aisle.

Lisa stared after him. *What on earth was that all about? Normally Ben stays as far away as possible from emotional contact, so why does he suddenly feel the need to interfere now? What makes it any of his business, anyway? Oh, forget it. I can't start worrying about him, too,* she decided. She shook her head and returned her attention to Prancer. Whatever was on Ben's mind, it obviously had something to do with Carole. And Carole was the last person Lisa felt like thinking about right then.

FOURTEEN

"I love Fridays!" Stevie declared, spreading her arms wide and tipping her face up to the sun. Belle snorted and tossed her head before breaking into a canter and then taking a few skittering steps to the side.

Emily and Callie laughed as Stevie struggled to maintain her balance and gather up her reins once more. "Good thing Max isn't here right now," Emily teased, urging Patch, the gentle pinto she was riding, into a trot to keep up. "He'd have a few things to say about your riding position."

Stevie playfully stuck her tongue out at Emily as Callie, who was riding PC a few yards away, grinned. "Well, Max isn't here, is he?" Stevie said tartly. She gestured at the peaceful meadow they were crossing to punctuate her point. "Anyway, if you're not nice to me, I won't tell you my exciting news. Then you'll be sorry."

"She's sorry, she's sorry," Callie said. "Come

on, don't keep us in suspense any longer. What's your big news?"

Stevie settled back in the saddle, feeling very pleased with herself. The three girls had just set out on a leisurely trail ride—Emily's idea, since she said getting out on the trail would be the best thing to help get Callie back in the swing of her rehabilitation work now that Sheila had been gone for two days. Stevie suspected that Emily herself was just in the mood for a good trail ride, but either way, she'd been happy to be dragged along. She had planned to do some work on Belle's extended trot in the indoor ring, but it was another gorgeous Indian-summer day, cold weather would be there before long, and Stevie had never been one to resist an afternoon of fun.

"Okay, since you asked nicely, I'll tell you," Stevie said, relenting. "We're on again!"

"You mean for A.J.?" Emily looked interested. "Go on."

Stevie had to pause to drag Belle's nose away from some tasty-looking weeds. The mare was allergic to some plants, so Stevie had to be extra diligent whenever they were out on the trail. A moment later Belle was trotting forward again, and Stevie continued. "Phil set the whole thing up with A.J.'s parents. They're dragging him to some relative's eightieth birthday party—there's no way he's getting out of that one—and we're all going to be there waiting for him when they get back." She grinned proudly, certain that the plan would succeed. "He won't be able to escape this time. He'll have no choice but to talk to us."

Callie pursed her lips. "I don't know about that," she said cautiously. "But it does sound promising, I'll give you that."

"Definitely." Emily looked excited. "It's brilliant, Stevie."

"You'll both come, won't you?"

Callie looked amused. "We might," she teased. "But only if you tell us when it is."

"Oops!" Stevie grinned sheepishly. "Sorry about that. It's tomorrow. The party's in the morning, so we'll gather around lunchtime."

"Great!" Callie declared immediately. "Count me in. It'll be the perfect excuse—Scott's been threatening to drag me to the Willow Creek High football game tomorrow afternoon."

Emily was frowning. "I can't make it," she said, sounding disappointed. "My folks are taking me out to lunch in D.C. I'm not sure what the big occasion is, but they've been really insistent about it, so I don't think they're going to want to reschedule. I can ask, but you probably shouldn't count on me."

Stevie frowned. She *had* been counting on Emily. She'd been counting on everyone coming and doing their part to help get through to A.J. But then she shrugged. It couldn't be helped.

"Okay. We'll miss you," she told Emily. "But we'll let you know how it goes." She gathered her reins and clucked to Belle. "Now come on. Last one to the woods is a rotten egg!"

The next day, Phil was waiting at the edge of the road when Stevie and Alex arrived to pick him up. Stevie eased the car to a stop and kept the engine idling.

"Hi," Phil said, leaning through the open window to give her a quick kiss. Then he hurried around to the passenger side, where Alex hopped out to let him into the backseat of the two-door car.

As soon as both guys were safely inside, Stevie gunned the motor. She was eager to get to A.J.'s house and get this intervention started.

Alex cast her a dubious glance. "Are you sure you don't want me to drive the rest of the way?"

Stevie ignored him. He'd been complaining about her driving throughout the twenty-minute ride from Willow Creek. "Is everything set?" she asked Phil.

"Pretty much," he replied. "I spoke to Mr. Mc-Donnell this morning before they left. After the party, they're going to take Elizabeth shopping over in Berryville. That way they can drop A.J. off at home, and we'll have him all to ourselves for an hour or two."

Stevie nodded grimly. She hoped they wouldn't need that long, but she was glad they had it.

Less than five minutes later, her tires were crunching over the gravel surface of A.J.'s driveway. Scott's green sports car was already parked in front of the garage, and Scott and Callie were leaning against it. "Won't he be suspicious when he sees all our cars in front of his house?" Stevie commented, glancing at Phil in the rearview mirror.

"Good point." Phil nodded. "Why don't you pull around the corner and leave it behind that clump of trees? He'll never notice it there."

Alex hopped out of the car. "I'll tell Scott to do the same."

Stevie hardly heard them. She had just noticed Callie's face. It looked as tortured as Stevie had ever seen it. Beside her, Scott was looking uncharacteristically grim. "Can you move the car?" she asked Phil distractedly. "I've got to talk to Callie."

"Uh, sure." Phil looked confused, but Stevie ignored him. She hurried over to Callie just as she swung away from the car on her crutches. Scott gunned the motor loudly a few times, waiting for Phil to pull out from behind him. As soon as Stevie's car was out of the way, he sped backward into the street.

"Callie?" Stevie peered into the other girl's face. Callie looked positively miserable. Her eyes were red, and her normally creamy complexion looked washed out and blotchy. "Callie, what's wrong?"

Callie blinked. For a moment she didn't answer, as if Stevie's appearance had taken her completely by surprise. "Hi, Stevie," she said at last. "What's wrong is that I'm a total idiot."

"What are you talking about?"

"It's Sheila." Callie took a deep breath and ran a hand through her blond hair. Her voice sounded strangely hollow. "It turns out she isn't such a great friend after all. We just found out this morning when the paper came."

"The paper?" Stevie felt confused. "You mean the newspaper? Did something happen to Sheila on her way home the other day?"

"Nope. Something happened *after* she got home," Callie corrected. "What happened was that Sheila took all the private things I told her while she was here and wrote a tell-all article for our local paper."

Stevie gasped. "You're kidding!" she said. "What did she write?"

"See for yourself," Scott said from behind her.

Stevie whirled around. She hadn't even noticed that Scott and Phil had returned from moving the cars. Now Phil was busy unlocking the McDonnells' front door with his borrowed keys and Scott

243

was gazing seriously at Stevie with a folded newspaper in his hand.

"Scott," Callie protested, sounding embarrassed. "Don't. I told you not to bring that. Everybody doesn't need to see it. Not now—it's not what we're here for."

Scott shrugged. "Everybody's going to see it soon enough." He sounded angry, and when Stevie took the paper from him and glanced at the masthead, she started to realize why.

"This isn't some local paper," she said slowly. "It's *The Washington Post*."

"The national wires picked it up after it ran in the Valley Vista paper yesterday," Scott explained. "The papers around here were all over it, especially since Dad just agreed to chair that controversial new welfare-reform committee."

"But what did she write?" Stevie was still having trouble comprehending what had happened. "I mean, what could you have possibly told Sheila that would matter to anyone else? It's not like you're on that committee with your dad."

"You don't understand." Scott took the paper back and flipped through the pages, folding it in the middle of the section before handing it back. "When you're in the public eye like my father is, just about everything about you—or your family—is interesting to somebody."

Stevie gulped as a headline leaped out at her

244

from the page: "Forester Family Flounders in Capital."

She read on, her heart sinking more with every line. The article started off straightforwardly enough, describing Congressman Forester's rise through the state government to the U.S. House of Representatives and his family's subsequent move to the Washington, D.C., area. It mentioned his recent work with the welfare committee Callie had mentioned, then went on to explain Sheila's role as a close, intimate friend of the family's.

Then the article took a sudden turn for the worse. Sheila went on to repeat what could only be Callie's most confidential comments. She described Callie's fears about moving across the country and meeting new people. She outlined all the ways that Callie found Willow Creek lacking as compared to her old hometown on the West Coast, and also made some insinuating comments about some "local bruiser" Callie had loved and left behind in Valley Vista. She listed all the unflattering comments the congressman had made about the people who had voted for him and his legislative colleagues, and made it sound as though he'd only joined the new welfare committee to forward his political career. She even described, in great detail, a drinking binge that she claimed Scott had gone on a year before. The story went on and on in that vein, spilling more and more of the Foresters' family secrets in stark black and white.

"Wow," Stevie said with feeling when she had read every horrible word. She glanced up at Callie and Scott. "Your dad must be furious."

"He is," Scott admitted. "Only in private, of course. But if Sheila so much as shows her face on the East Coast anytime soon, he'll probably strangle her."

"He won't get a chance," Callie said quietly. "He'll have to stand in line behind me."

FIFTEEN

Stevie swallowed hard. It was difficult to believe that anyone could be as devious, as sneaky and two-faced and downright despicable, as Sheila had been. Still, Stevie had to admit that she herself had to accept some blame for this situation. If she hadn't pushed Callie to confide in Sheila, this never would have happened.

"Callie," she began tentatively, "I'm so sorry. This is all my fault."

"No," Callie protested. "Stevie, please. I—I don't really want to talk about this right now."

"But you must be furious." Stevie took a step closer, wishing Callie would meet her eye. "I know I would be if someone betrayed me that way. And I feel terrible for what I did to make this happen."

"You don't understand." Callie bit her lip and shook her head. "You didn't do anything wrong, Stevie. This is my fault."

Stevie's jaw dropped. *"Your* fault?" she cried.

"You've got to be kidding. You *definitely* didn't do anything wrong. All you did was trust someone who didn't deserve it."

"I know," Callie said quietly, staring at the gravel beneath her feet. "And if I were an ordinary girl with an ordinary life, you'd be absolutely right to say that I hadn't done anything wrong. But I don't have an ordinary life, and I should have known better."

"What are you talking about?"

Callie fidgeted, her fingers running lightly over the smooth metal of her crutches. "I live in a fishbowl, Stevie. My whole family does. Maybe I was trying too hard to forget that recently. It's been so great just hanging out with you and your friends, acting like a regular sixteen-year-old and not worrying about public opinion for a change—"

"But just because your dad's a congressman doesn't mean you're any different than anyone else," Stevie argued. "You still have a right to live a normal life."

"A normal life?" Callie smiled ruefully. "I don't even know what that is, not really." She sighed. "It's nice to imagine what it must be like. But my life isn't like that, and I might as well accept it."

Stevie wasn't sure what to say to that. It was a pretty depressing thought. Why should Callie have to suffer because of what her father did for a living? "It doesn't seem fair," she murmured.

"I know." Callie shook her head slowly. "But it's the way it is."

Suddenly Stevie realized that Scott was being awfully quiet. She turned to him, her heart sinking. Just because Callie wasn't pointing any fingers didn't mean her brother felt the same way. Stevie and Scott had just become friends again after being at odds for far too long. Had this ruined things between them once again?

She was relieved when Scott met her eye steadily. "Um, I guess I should apologize to you, too," Stevie said. "If I hadn't egged Callie on the way I did—"

"Forget it," Scott interrupted. "You couldn't know this would happen." He shot Callie a look. "The only person really at fault here is Sheila. Maybe my sister shouldn't have told her some of the things she did, but Sheila still didn't have to write that article."

Alex stuck his head out the front door. "Yo, what are you three doing out there?" he called. "Come on, let's plan our strategy. The others will be here soon."

"Coming," Stevie called. She glanced at Scott and Callie. "Do you want me to keep quiet about this or what?"

Callie exchanged a long look with her brother.

249

Then she shrugged. "There's not much point," she said heavily. She waved at the newspaper Stevie was holding. "It's not exactly top secret."

Stevie handed the newspaper to her. "Don't worry," she said, trying to sound reassuring. "Our friends will understand. You can trust them to stand by you through this."

Callie nodded, and the barest hint of a smile played across her lips. "Thanks. You know, it's funny. In spite of everything that's happened, I do know that there really are a few people I can trust, and most of them are right here in Virginia. Ironically enough, my accident taught me that. But I'm just starting to realize how important that is to me."

Stevie impulsively flung an arm around Callie's shoulders. "You're becoming pretty important to all of us around here, too, you know. I don't know what we ever did without you."

This time Callie's smile was stronger, though still tinged with a trace of sadness. "Thanks," she said again. "I guess that's the silver lining to all this. For the first time, I really feel like Willow Creek is my home."

Twenty minutes later, Lisa sat on the McDonnells' love seat with Alex and listened with half her attention as the others debated what to say to A.J.

when he arrived. Everyone was there except for Carole.

Lisa had been one of the last to arrive. She'd spent the morning shopping with her mother, who had dropped her off at A.J.'s house on her way to another of her frequent group therapy sessions. It was always a strain to be cheerful and supportive of her mother when they spent any significant amount of time together. But even now that she was gone, Lisa couldn't seem to relax. Her mind was still filled with worries about Prancer, and her attention was focused on the door as she waited with hostility and dread for Carole to walk in.

Lisa forced her gaze away from the door and glanced around at the worried faces of her friends. Two of the faces looked even more worried than the others, and for a moment Lisa's conscience pricked her about feeling so sorry for herself when Callie and Scott had at least as many problems as she did right then. Scott had showed everyone that terrible newspaper article a few minutes earlier, explaining what had happened.

It must be awful to have all your secrets revealed to the world like that, Lisa thought, watching Callie out of the corner of her eye. *Especially by someone you thought you could trust . . .*

Her thought was interrupted by Stevie's loud

exclamation of dismay. She was staring at her watch, looking annoyed.

"Where in the world is Carole?" she cried. "If she doesn't get here soon, she'll miss the whole thing."

Lisa bit her lip and glanced down at her lap. Having Carole miss this little gathering didn't sound so bad to her.

"Maybe she lost track of the time," Phil suggested.

Stevie jumped to her feet. "That's it," she declared. "I'm calling Pine Hollow."

She grabbed the phone off the table near the couch and punched in the number. Tapping her foot, she waited for someone to pick up. "Hello?" she barked a moment later. "Who's this? Oh, hi, Ben. Is Carole around?"

Lisa twisted her hands nervously in her lap, listening silently along with everyone else as Stevie explained the situation to Ben. She couldn't help wishing that this whole day were over with already. It looked to be a pretty unpleasant proposition all around: First she would have to put up with Carole's sulky glances and the memory of what she'd done; then there would be the intervention itself, which was certain to be awkward at the very least. She sighed. *Who ever said weekends are supposed to be fun and relaxing?* she wondered.

———

Carole glanced over her shoulder at Ben as she rang the doorbell. "I told you we didn't have to rush over here like this," she said rather grumpily. "I bet A.J. isn't even here yet. Besides, there are plenty of other—"

She broke off what she was saying as Stevie flung the door open. "It's about time," Stevie greeted her brusquely. She did a double take when she noticed Ben hovering behind Carole, but she didn't say a word about his presence. "Come on in. He's not here yet."

Carole followed her inside. She still couldn't figure out why Ben had suddenly decided to come along. *I mean, he hardly even knows A.J.,* she thought irritably. *And if he weren't so gung ho about this intervention all of a sudden, I could have finished trimming Samson's tail instead of dropping everything and rushing over here.* She glanced at Stevie's back, feeling frustrated and petulant.

For her part, Stevie was feeling better as she led the two newcomers into the living room, where they joined the others. At last the intervention was back on track. She was more than a little surprised that Ben had come along. As far as she knew, he had only met A.J. a few times. Besides, he couldn't stand Scott, and he barely seemed to tolerate most of the rest of them other than Carole. *Still, the more the merrier,* she told herself.

As everyone settled in to wait for A.J. to arrive,

Stevie took up a position near the window, keeping one eye on the road leading to the house and the other on Ben. Sure enough, he looked as ill at ease as she had ever seen him. He was hovering as close as he could get to the door without actually fleeing through it, and he scowled every time he looked at Scott. Although maybe that was her imagination, Stevie decided after a moment, because he seemed to be scowling an awful lot at Lisa, too.

Suddenly Ben turned and met her eye. Stevie quickly averted her gaze, fearing he had felt her staring at him. She knew he could be pretty sensitive . . .

"Hi, Stevie," he greeted her as he joined her by the window.

She smiled. "Hi. Thanks for coming to the intervention," she said. "It's nice of you to want to help A.J."

Ben hesitated, looking uncertain. "Uh, that's only one of the reasons I came," he said. "I was actually hoping to—"

"Stevie!" Julianna exclaimed, rushing over at that moment. "I just thought of something. Do you think I should wait in the other room at first? I mean, you know, because seeing me might make him feel weird or . . ."

Stevie turned to reassure the other girl. When she finished, to her surprise, Ben was still standing there, gazing at her intently. "Oh," she said. "Um, what were you saying?"

"Just that there's something I think someone should—"

This time Stevie interrupted him herself with an excited, slightly nervous yelp. She had just caught a flash of motion out of the corner of her eye. A car was approaching—Mr. McDonnell's car. "He's here!" she cried excitedly. "Here he comes!"

Forgetting all about Ben, she rushed to Phil's side. "Ready for this?" Phil asked grimly.

"Ready as I'll ever be." Stevie rubbed her hands together, feeling jittery.

"Okay." Phil took charge, his face and voice serious as he addressed the room. "Let's not rush to the door. We don't want to scare him off. Just hang here and let him find us. Okay?"

Everyone nodded. They waited silently for several seemingly endless minutes, until finally they heard the front door swing open. A moment later A.J. came into view. He spotted them immediately and stopped short, looking startled.

"What's going on?" he asked, a perplexed expression crossing his face.

Phil took a step forward. "A.J.," he said. "We're here to talk to you. All of us"—he swept an arm to indicate everyone present—"all of your friends are worried about you."

A.J. shrugged and averted his eyes from Phil's steady gaze. "There's nothing to worry about," he muttered.

"Come on, A.J." Phil took another step toward his friend. "We care about you. That's why we're here. We want to help. But first you have to tell us what's bugging you these days."

A.J. looked up, his brow furrowed into a scowl. "Is that what this is supposed to be?" he demanded, his voice tinged with sarcasm. "Some kind of big confessional moment, like on TV?"

"We're just trying to help," Stevie said as soothingly as she could.

"That's right," Alex added. "You can trust us."

A.J. ignored them. He was glaring at Phil. "You're way out of line here, old buddy," he said evenly.

"Look." Phil's voice was steady, though Stevie could see that he was trembling slightly. "We're out of other ideas. You won't talk to anyone, and—"

"That's right!" A.J. shouted, backing up a few steps into the hall. "Did you ever think it's because I don't *want* to talk to anyone? Because nobody could possibly understand what I—" He broke off suddenly and whirled around, racing for the stairs before anyone else could move. Seconds later there was the faint slam of a door from the second floor.

Julianna was the first to react. "A.J., wait!" she sobbed, taking off after him.

"Julianna . . ." Phil hurried after her. A moment later both of them had disappeared up the stairs in A.J.'s wake.

There was a moment of silence. "Wow," Scott said at last, taking a few steps out into the hall and peering up the stairs. "That didn't go quite the way I was expecting."

Alex walked forward to join him. "No kidding," he said wryly. "What should we do?"

"We'd better sit tight for now," Stevie said reluctantly. Even though every fiber in her being was screaming for action, she knew that Phil and Julianna would have a better chance of coaxing A.J. out of his room on their own than they would with a whole crowd trying to help. *Maybe this whole intervention thing was a mistake,* she thought. *Maybe seeing all these people scared him, made things worse . . .*

She shook her head briskly. That kind of thinking wasn't going to do anyone any good, least of all her. To distract herself, she wandered over to the sofa, where Lisa and Callie had perched nervously.

"Maybe Phil can convince him to give us a chance to help him." Lisa was obviously trying to sound optimistic but was failing miserably.

"Maybe," Stevie said. She took a seat between

the other two girls. Leaning back wearily against the sofa cushions, she glanced around the room. Alex and Scott were still standing near the stairs, looking worried, clearly still talking about A.J.'s dramatic exit. Carole was over near the windows, chattering intently at Ben, who listened without contributing much. Stevie couldn't quite hear what they were talking about, but she was pretty sure she picked up the name Samson once or twice. *It figures,* she thought. *Carole's attention never leaves that stable for long.*

She returned her own attention to Lisa and Callie. "Maybe we should have seen this coming," she commented. "If A.J. wouldn't talk to his family or Phil about whatever's bugging him, why should we think he'd talk to all of us?"

Callie glanced over at her quickly, wondering if the irrepressible Stevie was actually giving up. "I still think this intervention was a good idea," she said. "Talking to A.J. one-on-one wasn't going anywhere, right? It was time to try something new."

Of course, sometimes trying something new can backfire, Callie thought, flashing back to her own recent experience with Sheila. *Look what it got me and my family. Dad's in big trouble with his welfare committee, not to mention looking like a jerk in front of the whole country, especially the voters back home. Everyone at school is probably going to think*

Scott is some kind of alcoholic. And as for me . . .
She shuddered as she thought about how her life would be changed by the article's revelations. Now everyone would look at her and know just how cowardly and insecure she really was. She didn't know how she would be able to stand it. *At least Mom was mostly spared,* she thought ruefully, although she knew that was only partly true. Mrs. Forester would feel every ounce of her husband's and children's humiliation. That was the kind of person she was. *Still, it's a good thing I didn't remember to tell Sheila about Mom's "friendship" with that lawyer back home . . .*

She pushed that unwelcome thought out of her mind. "Anyway, it was worth a try," she went on aloud, referring both to the intervention and, privately, to the experiment with Sheila. No matter how painful the whole thing had been—and would be for the foreseeable future—at least it had taught Callie a few things, good and bad. It had taught her how deceitful some people could be, and who her real friends were. And it had taught her that she might as well stop clinging to the idea of "back home." That was an especially valuable lesson, because it had finally opened her eyes to the fact that she was still holding back, still refusing to admit that she was in Willow Creek for good, with no safety net waiting to catch her if it didn't work out. The thought was a little scary, but exciting, too, since it meant she was finally free to throw herself wholeheartedly into her new life here.

I can do it, she told herself, *and I have to do it. There's no other way.* She felt some of her natural grit and determination start to seep back. Those qualities had carried her successfully through thousands of miles of tough competition and even tougher terrain in countless endurance rides. Now she would have to trust them to give her the endurance to make it past this new challenge as well.

Still, she couldn't help feeling a bit depressed as she thought of the road ahead. She knew that some things would never change. She could never really escape her role as a member of a high-profile family, no matter how determined she was or how many miles she rode. It wouldn't be easy to forget that again anytime soon . . .

Lisa couldn't help noticing that Callie looked rather meditative and wistful, but she tactfully avoided mentioning it. "I think we have to keep trying to reach A.J. no matter how much he resists," she said instead. "He's hurting, he's our friend, and we have to try our best to help him. That's what friends are for, right?"

She glanced across the room at Carole as she said it. As she did, she felt that now familiar flash of anger, though it was noticeably weaker now. She still wasn't even close to forgiving Carole for what she had done, but now that her first flush of fury was fading, she was feeling more hurt than anything else. How could Carole have kept something so important from her? Were they really still as close as they'd always been, or had something changed without Lisa's noticing it? Was she being naive to think that she and Carole and Stevie could remain the kind of friends they had been in their younger days, the kind of friends who would do anything for each other without a second thought, the kind who told each other absolutely everything?

At that thought, she glanced involuntarily at Alex, who was still deep in conversation with Scott. Thinking about secrets reminded her that there was still one very important secret standing between her and Alex. She knew she had to do something about it soon, before too much more time passed. But today just didn't seem to be the day to think about that, not when so many other things were still up in the air . . .

Stevie caught Lisa's anxious glance at Alex and wondered about it. Was Lisa thinking about her promise to tell him her secret? *Probably not*, Stevie told herself quickly. *That's probably the last thing on her mind, between worrying about A.J., Prancer, and her fight with Carole.*

She supposed she couldn't blame Lisa for that. Stevie had a lot more urgent worries on her own mind at the moment than her brother's love life. Concern for A.J. was gnawing away steadily at her insides with every passing moment that Phil and Julianna remained upstairs. Was he ever going to tell them what was wrong? It seemed impossible that he wouldn't. Then again, when she thought back, it seemed impossible that things had come this far, lasted this long. She wasn't sure how much longer she could stand it.

She also wasn't sure how much longer she could stand watching Carole and Lisa shoot bitter looks at each other. The three girls had weathered fights in the past, but for some reason this one felt different. Maybe that had something to do with the way Carole and Lisa had each acted when the truth came out. Or maybe it was because they were all still getting used to Lisa's being back home after her long summer away . . .

Feeling Callie shift her weight on the sofa beside her, Stevie glanced over, noting the other girl's pensive face. Despite Callie's and Scott's assurances, Stevie still felt at least partially responsible for the whole Sheila fiasco. She also felt more than a little foolish. She didn't consider herself a gullible or unrealistic person—far from it—but she never would have guessed that anything like this could happen. *And now Callie and her family are paying for that,* she thought sadly.

Not wanting to think about that particular subject any longer, she glanced around the crowded room, her gaze finally settling on Carole. She was standing near the window with Ben, but the two of them weren't talking at the moment. Ben was staring at the ground, looking as if he wished he were somewhere else—a familiar position and expression for him.

Carole's expression was harder to interpret. Stevie narrowed her eyes, taking in her friend's furrowed brow, the fingers nervously twisting the ends of her hair the way they so often did when Carole was feeling conflicted or guilty about something. *She's probably just worrying about her fight with Lisa,* Stevie told herself. *Or she could be feeling bad about what just happened with A.J.*

Either or both of those possibilities made perfect sense, but for some reason Stevie wasn't quite satisfied. Carole's face tended to reflect her every thought and feeling, and Stevie had years of experience in reading it. Somehow, her expression right then seemed different, seemed *off* somehow. *Could something else be bothering her?*

Suddenly Carole turned to Ben and started talking, waving her hands around urgently, and that odd, anguished expression was gone. Stevie blinked, wondering if she had imagined the whole thing. This situation with A.J. was putting them all on edge. . . . Her gaze wandered back to

Ben. He looked perfectly miserable, and she strongly suspected it had nothing to do with A.J.

Why can't he just loosen up? she wondered. Remembering his pathetic attempt at conversing with her a little earlier, she shook her head with a mixture of contempt and pity. *Maybe if he didn't act like such a weirdo all the time, he'd be happier.*

She sighed, glancing at the stairs. There was still no sign of A.J., or of Phil and Julianna, either.

Of course, Ben's not the only one who needs help. I can think of a few other people in desperate need of an attitude adjustment right about now. Stevie glanced at Lisa and then back at Carole. Next her gaze traveled to Callie, and she was reminded again of deceitful Sheila. *Why don't people ever seem to act the way I think they should?* she wondered, turning her attention back to the still-empty stairs. *It sure would make life a lot easier.*

ABOUT THE AUTHOR

Bonnie Bryant is the author of more than a hundred books about horses, including the Pine Hollow series, The Saddle Club series, Saddle Club Super Editions, and the Pony Tails series. She has also written novels and movie novelizations under her married name, B. B. Hiller.

Ms. Bryant began writing The Saddle Club in 1986. Although she had done some riding before that, she intensified her studies then and found herself learning right along with her characters Stevie, Carole, and Lisa. She claims that they are all much better riders than she is.

Ms. Bryant was born and raised in New York City. She still lives there, in Greenwich Village, with her two sons.

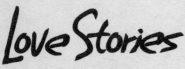